HAWK
A Lords of Carnage MC Romance

DAPHNE LOVELING

Copyright © 2017 Daphne Loveling
All rights reserved.
ISBN-13:
978-1546492856

ISBN-10:
1546492852

This book is a work of fiction.

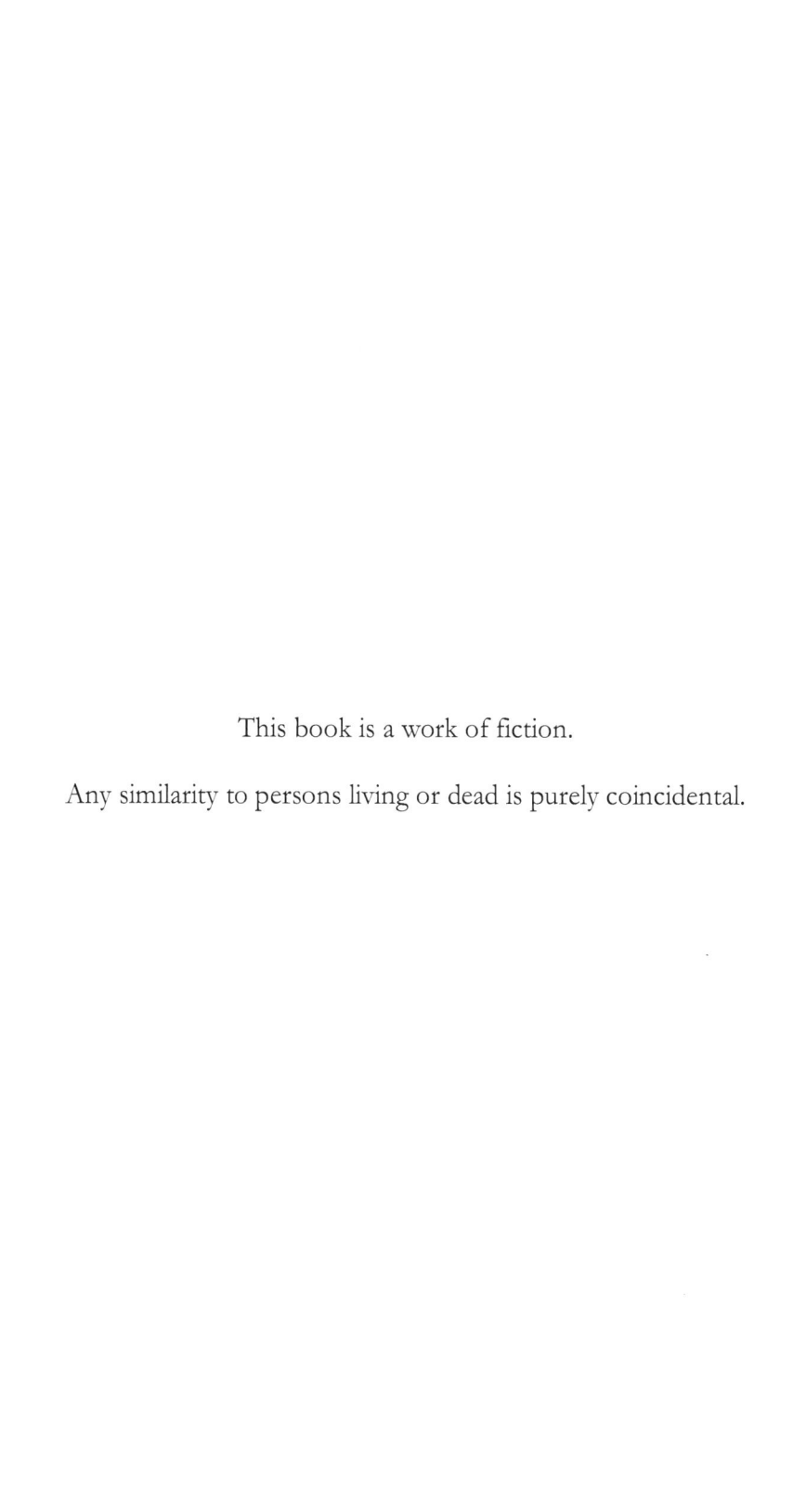

Any similarity to persons living or dead is purely coincidental.

To the super-supportive, rock star ladies of my ARC team.
You are the best.

Chapter 1

SAMANTHA

This is, without question, the weirdest professional gig of my life.

And as a freelance photographer who once shot a complete set of obedience school graduation pictures for a poodle and a corgi, that's saying something.

Maybe the weirdest thing of all is that it shouldn't be all that weird.

I mean, after all, it's just a wedding. And not even a dog wedding. Just a normal human wedding.

But normal is the absolute last thing this is.

* * *

I got this gig the way I've gotten many of my jobs since I moved to Tanner Springs five months ago: chance and word of mouth. One definite advantage of living here is there aren't a lot of professional photographers in a town this size. So when I tell people I meet what I do for a living, they're often really excited to meet me and ask me about my services, either for themselves or for someone else.

In this case, I was at Wee Haven KinderCare doing a shoot when I met Jenna Abbott. Wee Haven had hired me to do some new publicity photos for their website and promotional materials. A lot of photographers don't like to work with little kids, but personally, I think it's a blast. Sure, it's definitely more challenging than older kids and adults, but some of the best photos I've ever taken have been of children doing something that I'm actually trying *not* to get them to do. So, I've learned to just go with the flow, take a ton of pics, and trust in serendipity.

One of the little kids at Wee Haven I just couldn't stop photographing was a little nugget named Mariana. She was around a year old, with long, wavy blond hair and the most beautiful sunny, heart-melting smile. Little Mariana was just learning how to walk, and it was just about the cutest thing I had ever seen. I snapped way too many pics of her toddling around unsteadily on her chubby little legs, her hair catching a stray beam of sunlight shining in through the window. She was one of the most photogenic kids I'd ever met — a fact I made sure to mention to her mother when I had her sign the release forms to use Mariana's photos.

"Oh, gosh, thanks!" The mother, who told me her name was Jenna, blushed when I shook her hand.

"I'm serious," I told her. "Quite honestly, Mariana could easily find work as a child model. Or even an actor."

"Oh, wow. Thanks, but… I'm not sure I see myself as a hard-driven stage mom," she said, wrinkling her nose. "It sounds kind of… gross, actually."

I grinned. "I know what you mean. But I thought I should mention it, anyway. Mariana is a natural." I pulled up some of the shots of her on the screen of my digital camera so Jenna could take a look. "See what I mean?"

Jenna's eyebrows went up as I flipped through the images. "Those *are* really good. Even the candid shots are just beautifully framed and lit." She tilted her head at me, a curious look in her eye. "Do you do weddings?"

"Of course," I said immediately. I reached into my back pocket for one of my business cards. "There's a whole gallery of wedding photos on my website, if you want to take a look."

Jenna took the card without looking at it. "No need," she shrugged with a wide smile. "Just from looking at these shots of Mariana, I can already tell you're twice as good as any of the other photographers I've been considering. How much do you charge?"

I explained my rates to her, and said that since I was relatively new in town I was discounting some of my services to get my name out there and established.

"Oh, my God, that's so *reasonable*," she said, wide-eyed. "I can't believe you're the best photographer I've found and also the cheapest. Oh!" Her look changed to one of dismay. "But what if you're not available on the day! Oh, my God, *please* tell me you're free next month on the thirteenth!"

I reached into my back pocket again, this time for my phone. "I don't think I have anything then," I frowned, "But let me take a look."

A quick consult with my calendar told me that I was indeed free. Relief flooded Jenna's features. "Oh, thank God. Well, you're not free anymore," she said firmly. "Put me down right now. Jenna Abbott. Soon to be Watkins."

"Congratulations, Jenna." I tapped her name into my calendar and pressed save. "You're in."

* * *

The wedding day didn't start out all that strangely. I mean, sure, Jenna warned me things might be a little "unconventional." Apparently, the groom is the Sergeant at Arms (whatever that means) of the local motorcycle club in town, The Lords of Carnage. I have to admit, the name of the club did kind of give me some pause, even though I tried to play it cool.

"It'll be a simple ceremony," Jenna told me when we met at one of the coffee shops to talk over what she wanted. "The president of the club — Rock — is going to marry us. The wedding and reception are going to be outside, at one of the other guys' farms outside of town." She took a sip of her coffee. "Mostly, I just want a few posed shots, and then someone to be there to take photos that document the rest of the day," she said.

Usually, when brides say they want "simple," they don't really mean it. Like, they mean *only* four bridesmaids instead of seven, or *only* two-hundred people instead of the original four-hundred that her mom wants. But in Jenna's case it was clear to me she meant what she said. She showed me pictures of her dress, which was a simple but beautiful white sheath. "I don't have bridesmaids with matchy-matchy dresses or anything like that," she laughed. "We're just going to have Mariana and my son Noah stand up with us. The ceremony will be pretty short, and like I said, it's outside at Geno's farm. There's not going to be too much in the way of decoration. It's just a short ceremony, and then a long party."

"Sounds ideal," I murmured. I've never been much for big ceremonies myself. What Jenna was describing sounded a lot like what I would want for my own wedding. If I ever had any plans to get married, that is. Which I definitely do not.

Jenna asked me if I'd be okay staying through the reception so I could document the whole day. I assured her I was more than fine with that.

Then she hesitated for a moment.

"So…" she said slowly. "The club can get a little… *rowdy*, sometimes. But they're great guys, really, and it's all in good fun."

"No worries," I grinned. "How rowdy could it be?"

How rowdy, indeed.

Chapter 2
SAMANTHA

The address Jenna gives me to the farm is completely unfamiliar to me, so thank God for Google Maps. Unlike most weddings, where I visit the space before the ceremony and carefully choreograph the kinds of pictures they want before, during and after, Jenna didn't feel the need for all that preparation. "We'll get a few formal photos after the ceremony," she told me breezily when I suggested it. "Like I said, I just want you there to document the day. It will all work out."

Jenna, it must be said, is the single *least* bridezilla-y bride I have *ever* met.

When I arrive at the farm, there are already quite a few motorcycles and cars parked there, in the large front yard to the left side of the driveway. I pull my car off to one side, away from all the bikes, and open up the hatch. Grabbing the two bags holding my camera and other equipment, I sling the straps over one shoulder and slam the hatch shut. The farmhouse is set far back from the road, so I have a bit of a hike along the gravel driveway to get to it. But I'm used to lugging my stuff around.

As I come closer, I notice that there's already a crowd of maybe three or four dozen people gathered. Most of the men are dressed in jeans, motorcycle boots and leather vests sporting the logo of their motorcycle club and a variety of patches. It's like a sea of testosterone — bulging muscles, tattoos snaking up and down biceps, and hard jaws with varying degrees of facial hair. I square my shoulders and take a deep breath, forcing myself not to be intimidated. *You can do this, Sam,* I say to myself in my inner pep-talk voice. *You're the photographer. You're supposed to be here.*

Off to one side, I notice a man who must be the groom, judging from the way the others are circled around him. Cas, Jenna said his name is. He's *holy cow* gorgeous, with dark, thick hair that falls over his forehead and a close-cropped beard. He's standing in a group with five other men, and little Mariana's in his arms. The juxtaposition of this tattooed giant of a man holding a tiny blond girl should be jarring, but somehow, it isn't as weird as all that. Mariana is playing with the patches on his vest. As I watch them, Cas reaches over and carefully moves the single red rose pinned to where his boutonnière would be so she won't pull it off or stick it in her mouth.

I tear my eyes away from the scene, regretful that I don't have my camera out in time to capture the moment. I take a quick scan of the crowd to see what else I can notice right off about the wedding party. There are women here, too, of course, but my attention had been captured by the men first. Now, as I glance around, I see that they're mostly dressed in tight, revealing dresses and heels that are way too tall and spiky to be tromping around in the grass. Except for a handful of kids running around, the crowd looks more like they're waiting to get back into a bar after a fire alarm has gone off than a wedding party. But hell, I once photographed a wedding where everyone — including the bride, the groom, and the officiant — was dressed like late-era Elvis. So who am I to judge?

I look around for Jenna, but she's nowhere to be seen. I imagine she's in the house getting ready. I'm just about to walk over to see if I can find her when a big, burly, barrel-chested man approaches me.

"Hey, you must be the photographer," he grunts, nodding down toward my camera.

I smile. "Hi. I'm Sam. Samantha." I hesitate, then hold out my hand.

Burly guy shakes it carefully, and I can tell he's trying not to crush my fingers. "Rock," he says simply. "I'm the one doing the marrying."

"Oh." I glance at his leather vest, and notice a patch on it with the word "president."

"I'll have one of the women let Jenna know you're here," he continues, gesturing to a tall brunette in impossibly high heels. "We'll get started in a couple minutes."

"Got it." I set my equipment bag down and grab the lenses I'll be needing. The brunette teeters over to Rock, who murmurs a few words to her, and then turns toward the house. I busy myself with my light meters and check that everything's in working order. I'm just finishing up when Rock walks over to a small clearing and raises his voice.

"Okay, we're gonna get started," he calls. "Gather around, and make sure to make a path for the bride."

The crowd gathers around to stand in a half-circle in front of Rock, laughing and talking as they go. Many of the men have bottles of beer in their hands, and some of the women are drinking, too. This is definitely the most laid-back wedding I've ever been to. I raise my camera and sneak a few quick snaps of some of the more colorful characters, sinking into my role as documenter of what will be one of the most important days of Jenna and Cas's lives.

Off to the side of where the crowd has gathered sits a single chair. As I watch, one of the club members strides solemnly up to it, carrying an acoustic guitar. He's strikingly handsome, with deeply tanned skin, dirty blond hair, and tattoos covering most of the skin on his thickly muscled arms. Reflexively, I pull the focus back and take a few shots of the way his body moves, and the raw, masculine beauty of him.

Then, as I continue to snap, he sits down with the guitar and begins to play.

The music is not at all what you'd expect to come from a huge, moderately dangerous-looking man. The crowd hushes as his fingers strum and pluck out a beautiful instrumental that immediately draws all eyes and ears to him.

The melody is soft and haunting. I could swear I've heard somewhere before, but can't quite place it. For a moment I just stand there, captivated by its beauty, and by the quiet command of the man playing it. Then with a start, I realized I've stopped taking photos. *Stop daydreaming, Sam. You've got a job to do.*

Moving as unobtrusively as I can, I crouch down and begin snapping shots of the guitarist as he plays, doing my best to capture the magic of the moment. The click of the shutter is so quiet I'm the only one who can hear it, and I hold down the button and take dozens of pics in rapid succession, not wanting to miss one single moment.

Then, as I watch him from my safe, voyeuristic place behind the lens, the man glances up. His eyes, a deep, piercing hazel color, lock on the camera. On *me*.

A jolt of heat bursts through me, followed by a wave of embarrassment. Usually when my subjects look directly at the camera, it doesn't feel like anything personal. I know I'm safe and unimportant behind the lens. When people look at the camera, they're generally imagining the people who will eventually see the photo, and hoping like hell they won't end up looking like a weirdo. But *this* is *completely* different. It feels like the guitarist's gaze is boring right through the camera — like he's looking right at me. Even though I know that can't be the case. He's just looking at the lens, like anyone else. He's just realized he's being photographed. That's all there is to it.

But those *eyes*… they're just… *mesmerizing*. Dazedly, I lower the lens for a second. His gaze doesn't move at all. With a shock, I realize he really *is* looking at me.

I almost drop the camera, and start forward to stop it from hitting the ground. When I glance back up, I catch just the faintest shadow of a smile on his face. Then, almost like I imagined the whole thing, he looks back down at the guitar and continues to play.

My heart starts to hammer in my chest as I shakily raise the camera again and half-stumble to my feet. Part of it is the adrenaline rush from almost breaking my best camera. But most of it is from being caught so unaware — and somehow, feeling so *exposed* — by a simple look.

I take a deep breath and will myself to concentrate. This is the most important part of the wedding, and I owe it to Jenna not to screw it up. Pushing away my embarrassment, I move into position to photograph the groom's and bride's entrance.

I'm just in time to start shooting as Cas starts to walk down the makeshift aisle created by the parting of the crowd. Little Mariana is still on his hip, dressed in a tiny pink flowered sundress. Walking next to Cas, tiny hand engulfed in his larger one, is a little boy who must be their son Noah. The image is just priceless — I couldn't have done better if I'd posed them myself. I snap a few shots of the three of them from off to one side, switch lenses, then take a few steps forward and snap a few more. Mariana sees me and waves enthusiastically. The crowd looks over at me and laughs. I blush and wave back, then disappear behind the camera again. I try my best to be invisible when I'm working weddings.

Cas continues down the aisle, and a couple of the men slap him on the shoulder as he walks by. When he gets to Rock, the two of them shake hands. Cas leans down and says something to Noah.

"She's coming!" cries a female voice from the back.

Then, almost as one person, the crowd turns to face the house, where the bride has appeared.

Jenna walks through the crowd, her face radiant. She's paired her sheath dress with simple white flats. Her hair falls loose around her shoulders, with just a few tiny flowers arranged artfully toward the crown of her head. I'm snapping photos like a madwoman, not wanting to miss a single second. When she gets to the end and joins her little family, there's a look of such sweet, pure love between Cas and Jenna that a big lump of emotion rises in my throat. A wave of sadness hits me like my own personal tidal wave, but I force it aside. I don't have time to be letting this wedding get me thinking about the past. I'm a professional, and today is all about Jenna and Cas.

The hand that isn't holding Mariana take's Jenna's. She gives her groom a brilliant, dazzling smile. Then the four of them turn together to face Rock.

The ceremony itself is short and simple, like Jenna said it would be. Rock does a gruff but effective job of officiating. Jenna and Cas wrote their own vows, and as they both promise to love and cherish each other, I take advantage of the moment to get close-ups of both of them staring into the eyes of the person they are vowing to spend the rest of their lives with.

Honestly, as weird as this has been so far, it's also one of the most beautiful weddings I've ever been to.

At the end of the ceremony, Cas turns to another man behind him and hands Mariana off. He takes both Jenna's hands in his, and Rock's voice booms out over the crowd.

"Ghost Watkins, you may now kiss your bride."

My brow crinkles in confusion at the name Rock calls him, but I don't have time to wonder about it, because Cas is leaning forward. He pulls Jenna into his arms, tilting her head back toward his, and the kiss they exchange is so full of passion and love that I half-laugh, half-sob as I capture the moment.

For a couple of seconds, there's an almost reverent silence.

Then, a raucous cheer erupts from the crowd.

"HELL YES!" someone yells over the others. "Let's get this party started!"

Chapter 3
HAWK

Twenty minutes into the reception, I'm already taking bets with myself on how long the hot photographer is gonna last before she freaks out and runs away.

As soon as the wedding ends, I head into Geno's house to put away my guitar, before one of the men gets drunk and disorderly and does something stupid like use it for batting practice. It's not a very expensive guitar, but it has a lot of sentimental value. It's the only thing I have left of my older brother, who died when I was seventeen.

This morning, the brothers set up everything necessary for an epic party in the field behind Geno's house. At the club level, the preparations for this day have been going on for weeks. This is one of our brothers who's getting married, after all. And not just *any* brother, either. Ghost is our Sergeant at Arms — the man who keeps our club in order. Normally he'd be the one making sure things didn't get dangerously out of hand today, but as the groom he's officially off the clock, so all bets are off.

The whole point of today is to make goddamn sure that Ghost and Jenna start off their married life with a blowout that will be the stuff of club legend.

Our VP Angel, Ghost's best buddy and Jenna's brother, has had enough booze and food brought in for as long as the Lords can keep this party going. A bunch of long tables are set up in the middle of the field, probably by the prospects early this morning. A couple of the tables are laden with main and side dishes and desserts, courtesy of the old ladies and club girls, who make it a point of pride to feed their men well. Our enormous custom-made grill has been hauled here from the clubhouse, ready to be filled with steak and chicken for the men and women, and hamburgers and hot dogs for the kids. Off to the side, our smoker is emitting the fucking delicious smell of barbecue, expertly manned by Tank.

When I come back out of Geno's place, the huge sound system that Striker and Tweak set up is already blasting classic rock at a volume that's almost hard to believe. If Geno had anyone living close by, we'd be at risk of getting the cops called out here. But as it is, he's so far out of town there's no one anywhere near close enough to be bothered by us. Geno does not like neighbors. Or people in general, really.

The older kids have rounded up the younger kids to take them inside for their own party, a massive sleepover in Geno's basement. His man cave features a seventy-five inch flat screen TV, a game system, a popcorn machine, and more movies than any one man could watch in a lifetime. The kids will hang out and eventually crash there, leaving the adults to get on with their own craziness. Already, a bunch of the brothers have started to party in earnest. There's a few groups trading shots of whiskey over at one table. Some others are gathered over by the smoker trading stories and laughing their asses off. More than one has decided to skip the formalities and go straight for the pussy.

I've been watching the hot photographer since even before the wedding ceremony started. She is definitely not the kind of chick you usually see hanging around an MC. Not that our club girls and old ladies aren't hot. Shit, our women could compete with any women from any MC I've seen in terms of looks. But the photographer stands out among all of them, in more ways than one. For one thing, she's dressed differently, in a no-nonsense black button-down blouse and black pants. It's clear from her clothes she's trying not to be noticed, and I guess that makes sense. After all, I suppose it's tough to take pictures of people acting naturally when they're aware that you're watching them with a camera pointed at their every move.

The thing is, though, even with the inconspicuous clothes she's wearing, there's no way in *hell* this girl could ever be invisible. She's fucking gorgeous: long, straight, glossy chocolate-brown hair, a tiny waist that rounds out into full, luscious curves, and big, dark, doe-like eyes. It doesn't look like she's wearing any makeup, but Jesus, she doesn't need to. Her skin is absolutely perfect, her mouth full and pouty. As I watch her move unobtrusively around the crowd and snap pictures of Jenna, Ghost, and the others, her brow furrows in concentration and somehow it makes her even more beautiful. When she bites her lip while staring down at the screen of her camera, I want to bite it for her.

In my experience, people who've never been around the club before tend to be pretty fucking intimidated by us. And probably with good damn reason. So I watch in surprise and amusement over the next hour or so as this chick seems to barely acknowledge that *any* of the shit happening around her is anything but completely normal.

She takes tons of pictures of Ghost and Jenna, dutifully averting the lens whenever their kissing and groping starts to turn X-rated.

She moves in close to capture a shot of Beast — who's got to be almost two feet taller than her and weighs close to three times as much — as he downs half a bottle of bourbon in one go to win a bet with Gunner.

And she doesn't bat an eye when Tweak passes out first, and a few of the brothers decide to tie ropes around his bike and haul it up into a tree for him to find when he wakes up.

I'm staring in open admiration at her when Thorn comes up behind me, his eyes following my gaze.

"She's a ride, isn't she?" he says, his Irish brogue deepening as it always does when he's been drinking.

"That she is," I agree, chuckling appreciatively. "I've been thinking about riding her ever since she stepped foot onto the farm."

Which is true. My dick's been standing at half-attention for a while now, wondering if he's gonna be called into duty. I should leave the girl alone, though. She's just trying to do her job. And Jenna might be pissed if I scare away her wedding photographer.

Just then, Melanie, Rachel, and Tammy, three of the club girls, come over to where Thorn and I are standing. All three of them have progressed to the drunk and giggly phase.

"You've been ignoring us!" pouts Tammy, batting her heavily mascara'ed eyes first at Thorn, then me. She leans forward toward Thorn, but then stumbles on her high heels and falls clumsily against his chest.

"You've already had a bit of a craic, haven't ye?" Thorn laughs, setting Tammy to rights.

"What?" she asks, confusion twisting her pretty face. "I have not!"

Thorn snorts. "No matter, love. English is optional for what we're about to do." Before Tammy knows what's happening, Thorn's picked her up and swung her over his shoulder. She squeals in mock-protest, but pleasure is obvious in her voice.

"Careful not to shake her too hard," I call out with a laugh as he carries her off. "She's likely to spring a leak."

"So noted," he calls back.

Melanie and Rachel sidle up next to me expectantly. They look like twins, even down to what they're wearing. Both of them have a full cascade of almost white-blond hair — though Rachel's definitely isn't natural. I know from experience how good they are in bed, and that they really get off on giving a man a show together before moving on to the main event.

"So," Melanie purrs, running a long, lacquered nail down my chest. "You wanna come help us find someplace private? We're bored, and Rach was just saying how fun you are."

I'm not in the habit of turning down a little *fun*, especially not in the form of a threesome. But just as I'm opening my mouth to answer, I happen to glance over toward the tables of food. The hot photographer is standing there, camera raised, but she's not looking at the tables. She's looking at me.

Our eyes lock. She freezes, like a small animal caught in a hunter's rifle sight. For a second, neither one of us looks away. It's a repeat of earlier, when I caught her taking my picture playing guitar at the beginning of the wedding.

Then her eyes shift, taking in the girls as they hang on me. A slight look of disgust flashes across her features, and she looks quickly away, her lip curling a bit. Her whole demeanor stiffens, and she crouches down and goes back to her work, positioning the camera so as to take in the spread of food and some of the people laughing and eating in the background.

I don't know why I care. It's not like I'm all surprised that a nice little white-bread girl would be shocked or disgusted by what people in the club get up to. Outlaw MCs exist precisely because people like her look down at people like us.

But somehow, it kind of chaps my ass. She's been completely professional and hasn't batted an eye about anything all afternoon, and she then chooses *me* to have a fucking problem with.

For the next minute or so, she ignores me so completely that I almost fall for it. I almost mistake her act for indifference. But just as I'm about to leave with Melanie and Rachel and find us a private spot to fuck, I catch the photographer just barely turning her head toward us, and I realize she's sneaking a glance to see if I'm still there.

Then it hits me. Whatever she feels about me, it's sure as shit not indifference.

I should leave her alone, I tell myself for the dozenth time. Let her survive her brush with the wild side unscathed, and go back to photographing little kids' birthday parties or whatever she does most of the time.

But damned if I don't want to hear what her voice sounds like, and watch her bite that lip from close up. I want to see her skin flush as she pretends she hasn't been watching my every move.

It can't hurt anything to just go talk to her.

So, ignoring my better judgment and my better nature, I tell Melanie and Rachel I'll take a rain check, and head over to say hello.

Chapter 4
SAMANTHA

The tattooed guitarist detaches himself from the two blond bombshells and starts to amble toward me.

"Shit," I murmur under my breath. "Shit shit shit."

I thought I'd been doing a good job of avoiding the guitar player guy. After the weird whatever-that-was when we locked eyes at the beginning of the wedding, I felt so flustered that I didn't trust myself to take any more pictures of him, or even be around him. So I've been doing my best to give him a wide berth at the reception. But of course, in order to do that, I have to have some idea of where he is. Which means that I've been periodically scanning the crowd to keep tabs on him. It's been working perfectly well for a couple of hours now.

Except that when I did my last scan just now, he had his tongue halfway down the throat of one woman while another was sliding her hand down to his crotch.

And before I could manage to look away, his eyes were locked with mine again as I struggled to keep the shock and revulsion off my face.

He's already closed half the distance between us when I realize what's about to happen. Before I can even think what I'm doing, I've bolted from where I'm standing by the food table — hoping not to look like I'm running away and probably failing miserably.

I try to walk with purpose, like I've just seen a shot I need to capture. Unfortunately, the only thing in the direction I'm heading is the bar. So I make a beeline for that and lean against it, my breathing shallow and labored like I'm a drowning person who's just reached the life raft.

"Hey, can I get a gin and tonic?" I say nervously to the tall, pretty woman who's mixing drinks. "A double." Normally I don't drink on the job, but suddenly my nerves are jangling and I need something to calm myself down.

"Sure thing, honey," she says, eyeing me speculatively. I literally have to stop myself from drumming my fingers on the bar as she mixes it. When she finally hands it to me, I take the glass from her and gulp down a long swallow. Then I take a deep breath and turn around to scan for my next exit route.

"Glad to see you loosening up a little bit."

I shriek and almost dump my drink on his chest. Which would hardly be *my* damn fault if I did, because he is standing literally six inches in front of me.

"Jesus!" I sputter. "Haven't you ever heard of personal space?" My gin and tonic sloshes over the side of the cup onto my fingers. Shaking a little, I transfer the glass to my other hand and lick the liquid off them.

"I take it back," he chuckles. "Apparently it's gonna take more than a gin and tonic to loosen you up."

"I'm not *supposed* to be loosened up," I spit. "I'm supposed to be working."

I expect him to fling some cocky retort at me, but for a moment he doesn't say anything, just looks at me intently. With a start, I realize he's watching me as I suck the remaining splashes of gin and tonic from my fingers. I pull my hand away from my mouth self-consciously and blush.

"It's a party," he says. "In case you hadn't noticed." His voice softens a little, a bit of husk in his tone. "Pretty sure Jenna won't mind if you actually have a good time."

I glance over to where she and Cas are slow-dancing to the ballad that's playing on the sound system. Cas's hands are roaming over Jenna's ass, and their eyes are locked onto each other like there's no one else in the world.

"Maybe not," I admit. "But I do have a job to do. Jenna didn't hire me to sit around and drink. Besides," I say, nodding my head toward the Doublemint twins. "Don't you have enough company for one night?"

He laughs. "Them? Don't worry about Melanie and Rachel. They're just some of the club girls."

"What does that mean?" It sounds vaguely… prostitute-y.

"It means they hang around the MC, hoping one of us will put a ring on it." He flashes me a sexy grin and glances down at my camera. "Come on. Take a little break. I'm guessing you've taken enough pictures to fill forty wedding albums."

"And do what?" I shoot back at him.

"Get to know someone new." His grin grows wider, and becomes a challenge as he holds out his hand in a half-mocking gesture for me to shake it. I don't want to take it, but I don't want him to think he's rattling me, so I do anyway.

His touch feels like I've been jolted by a cattle prod. A burst of heat flames through me, immediate and unexpected. I audibly gasp, but I *think* I don't do it loud enough that he hears me over the music.

My mouth opens a little, my breath speeding up as heat and lust begin coursing through my veins.

He pulls me toward him during the shake, until I'm so close to him I can feel the heat of his skin. His scent is manly, musky with just a slight hint of whiskey. The few men I've been with haven't smelled anything like this. It's raw… intoxicating. "What's your name, sweetheart?" he rasps against my ear.

"Uh, it's *not sweetheart*," I retort, struggling to keep my composure. Shakily, I pull my hand away from his and take a step back. When I break contact, my skin instantly misses his. With my other hand, I raise my glass and take a big gulp of the gin and tonic.

He seems completely unfazed. "Well, then, give me something else to call you," he shrugs.

His tone is maddeningly reasonable. A wave of irritation washes over me. I've never met someone I was so instantly exasperated by and attracted to at the same time. And what's even more infuriating is, I'm almost certain he *knows* I'm attracted to him.

As if he can read my mind, he cocks his head and smirks at me. "Well?"

I *know* he's trying to get to me. He's trying to get me pull down my defenses. And damn it, it's working. I resist the urge to scream in frustration.

"I'm… Samantha," I choke out. No one calls me that except my grandmother, but for some reason right now it is *absolutely* important to keep some distance between us, however small.

He winks at me like he's not fooled. "Pleased to meet you, sweetheart," he drawls, his voice dipping into a low, sexy growl. "I'm Hawk."

I struggle against the fog of rage in my brain. The only defense I have against this man is sarcasm and mockery, I realize. So I use them.

"Hawk?" I snort, trying to knock him off balance. "What kind of a name is that?"

A slight frown crosses his features. I can't tell whether he's angry or amused. I feel a tiny zing of triumph.

"You don't like my name," he says in a tone I can't read. "I didn't insult *your* name."

To be honest, he doesn't seem in the least bit hurt. But even so, I still feel weirdly bad about making fun of him. And that makes me even madder, but also throws me a little.

I shrug, fighting the urge to apologize. "I didn't say I didn't like it."

"Oh, so you *do* like it," he smirks. "That's good."

Goddamnit, I've been played *again*. "Oh, my God!" I roll my eyes, exasperated. "I didn't say that either! Jesus, is there *any* way to have just a normal conversation with you?"

"You want a normal conversation?" He nods. "Go ahead."

I eye him suspiciously.

"What?" he asks, spreading his hands wide and feigning innocence.

I sigh. I don't know why I'm doing this. "Fine," I huff, and raise my glass to take another drink. "So. Hawk. Is that your real name?"

"Real enough. Besides," he continues, taking a long moment to rake his eyes over my body, "you'll like it a lot better when you're screaming it with my head between your legs."

I'm in the middle of swallowing, and some of the gin goes down the wrong pipe, making me start to gasp and splutter. Hawk reaches over to pound me on the back, but I wave him off.

"Do you… actually get results with that line?" I say in a strangled voice, when I can finally breathe again.

"Never used it before now," he murmurs, leaning in and speaking the words against my ear. "But it looks like I'm about to."

"Are you *kidding* me?" I cry, pulling back and rounding on him. "Sorry, I think you have me mixed up with someone who has no standards." Anger courses through me, or maybe that's the alcohol. It feels *good* to get mad at him. Like *I'm* the one in control.

I'm opening my mouth to go off on him when a shout from over toward the main crowd makes me turn my head.

"Hey, y'all!" calls a tall, handsome man with a thick blond beard. "It's time to drink a toast to the bride and groom!"

A bunch of people in the crowd whoop and yell in response. "Go for it, Angel!" one of the other men shouts.

"Shit, I have to go," I mutter, handing Hawk what's left of my drink. I head over to where the man called Angel is talking, fumbling with my camera as I go. I should have been paying attention to this. Now I can only hope his speech is long so I can get good light and some good shots before he's done.

"I don't mind tellin' y'all that it was a little bit of an adjustment for me when I learned that my best buddy and my baby sister were seeing each other," Angel begins. "Matter of fact," he chuckles, "seems to me I remember giving Ghost a piece of my mind, and my fist, when I found out."

The crowd turns to Cas and Jenna with a laugh. Cas raises his beer and nods at Angel with a grin. I move in at an angle and start snapping.

"But I gotta say, I can't think of anybody I'd trust more to be by Jenna's side. And Ghost, you're a lucky man to have someone like Jenna. I know she'll always love you and be the best mama to your kids she can be."

Some of the women *awww*, and a few of the men whistle. It is unexpectedly touching. I say unexpectedly because even though I have photographed plenty of weddings, I secretly don't like them very much. Chalk it up to personal history, maybe, but it's a little hard for me to believe in the "happily ever after" thing. From what I've seen in my twenty-three years, it's generally not much more than a fairy tale for people who prefer to live in hope instead of relying on experience.

But as Angel continues to talk about the couple, and I snap shots of how happy everyone is for them, I start to feel a little misty-eyed in spite of myself. *It's probably just the gin and tonic,* I tell myself crossly. I shouldn't have broken my rule and had that drink. Plus, unlike most weddings where the bartenders tend to water down the drinks, I think the bartender actually made mine *stronger* than normal. Dimly, I realize I've forgotten to eat the energy bar I tucked in my bag, and that as a consequence I haven't had any non-liquid calories in almost five hours.

I'm making a mental note to grab a hot dog or something to tide me over when I suddenly see the *perfect* angle for a photo. If I can just manage to get up on one of the large speakers behind Angel before he's done talking, I can get a shot of him making his toast in the foreground, with the perfect framing of the newlyweds in the background. Nothing makes me more excited than a well-timed picture, so I immediately head over and grab a folding chair, then move behind the speaker and use it to boost myself up.

The speaker is a little wobbly, like an old stepladder, but I'm not going to be up there for very long. The perfect angle for the shot will be with me crouching and off to one side, so I inch my left foot to the edge and lean out slightly. Just as Angel is holding up his beer to say the official toast, Jenna looks up at Cas in the background, and I refocus the lens and triumphantly start snapping the exact shot I was hoping to catch.

"To Jenna and Ghost!" Angel yells.

The crowd roars in loud approval. Then, someone somewhere starts the music up again. The loud boom of the first drumbeat coming from the speaker I'm standing on startles me, and before I can realize what's happening I've lost my balance and am falling backwards. My instinct to windmill my hands and catch onto something is overridden by my instinct to protect my camera, and before I know it I'm in free fall, desperately hoping whatever I come into contact with when I hit the ground won't hurt too badly.

There's a sickening moment when I'm airborne, my stomach in my throat.

And then I'm caught up in someone's strong, muscular arms.

I'm starting to breathe out a shocked sigh of relief, when an all-too familiar voice murmurs in my ear:

"Do I get bonus points for saving the camera?"

Chapter 5

HAWK

Days later, I can practically still smell the scent of her shampoo tickling my nose as I caught her in my arms, just before she hit the ground.

I could see right away that the speaker she was about to climb up on was wobbly and might not be safe for her to stand on, but I didn't want to yell at her and spoil Angel's toast. As she clambered up on top of it, I circled around behind the crowd to the other side, until I was standing right behind it. My plan at first was to hold onto the speaker for her and steady it as she took pictures, but the thing started to wobble backward before I could get to it. So instead, I just barely had time to put my arms out before she dropped right into them.

It happened so quickly she didn't even have time to yell or cry out. Being caught before hitting the ground surprised her into silence. But that didn't last long.

"Do I get bonus points for saving the camera?" I murmured in her ear.

The look of shock on her face turned to indignation when she realized it was me who'd caught her.

"Are you seriously following me around this reception?" she sputtered, her eyes wide.

"You're welcome," I grinned. Instead of letting her go, I tightened my grip on her just a little. She felt light in my arms, and one of her breasts was brushing against my chest. I took another whiff of her hair, and tried to decide whether to kiss her.

Samantha looked like she was trying to consider whether to scream at me or murder me. "You know, you could have broken your neck, climbing up on that shaky thing," I admonished her. "What the hell were you thinking?"

"None of your business what I was thinking," she bit out. "I was trying to capture an angle. I had a shot in mind. Which I *did* get, by the way."

"I think that gin and tonic has impaired your judgment," I said mildly. "Why didn't you ask someone to help you?"

"There wasn't time," she said impatiently. "I didn't know how long Angel was going to talk. Now, are you going to let me down?"

"Are you going to promise me you won't do anything like that again without asking for some help?" I tightened my grip on her just a little more, to show her I wasn't kidding around. It was cute that she was so mad, but frankly, she could have seriously hurt herself. The way she was falling, backwards like that without her hands out to protect her, she could be on her way to the emergency room right now. A belated spike of adrenaline shot through my veins, making me feel a little sick, and a little mad.

"I mean it sweetheart," I rasped, lowering my voice. My jaw tensed. "You almost cracked your fool head open. You're damn lucky I was there to catch you."

Samantha's brow knit in frustration. I was sure she was going to start kicking and screaming or something to get out of my arms. But then, just when I was about to give in and let her go, her plump bottom lip slid between her teeth.

That lip I was dying to bite.

My cock sprang to life, instantly rock hard.

"Okay," she half-whispered, her eyes barely meeting mine. "You're right. I could have gotten hurt." She was so close to me that I could see her pupils, wide and dark. As my eyes locked on hers, I could hear her breathing speed up. Her bottom lip escaped her teeth.

I suppressed a groan. My cock throbbed under my zipper. Jesus fuck, I wanted to crush her mouth with mine, carry her to the first flat surface and sink myself deep inside her. It hit me with so much force it almost felt like I'd been punched.

Why the fuck I didn't just go for it, I have no goddamn idea.

Instead, like a fucking fool, I set her down, stepped back, and nodded.

"That's better," I said gruffly.

Then I turned, walked away, and proceeded to get drunker than shit off a bottle of whiskey I grabbed from behind the bar.

When I woke up, it was after four in the morning, and someone had stuffed a wad of cotton in my mouth and taken a ball peen hammer to my skull. Samantha was gone by then, of course. And I haven't seen her since.

Not that I haven't wanted to. Hell, I've been thinking about her off and on ever since that night. Like now.

But I was lying when I said I wasn't sure why I didn't just go for it with Samantha. I know exactly why.

Because when I looked in those deep brown eyes, I *wanted* her. Wanted her so much I could taste it. Wanted to possess every inch of her body, to hear her call my name when she came.

Wanting is dangerous. When you want things, sometimes it makes you do stupid shit. You make mistakes.

If I need sex, I can get sex. The club girls are always around, and beyond that, I've never had to try too hard to attract women. I want the hot photographer, sure, but I don't *need* her. I can get my needs satisfied somewhere else. The *wanting* part is irrelevant. I've learned to ignore what I want. It's better that way.

* * *

"Is Ghost back yet?" Gunner asks me as he walks up to the bar.

"They just got back into town," I tell him, and signal Jewel for a beer. "Angel said he and Jenna went over to Skid's place to pick up the kids and bring them back home. Ghost should be here soon, once he gets done dropping them all off."

Ghost and Jenna just got back from their honeymoon: a five-day motorcycle trip that Ghost had planned as a surprise for his bride. He'd made all the arrangements himself — even down to getting Rena, Skid's old lady, to babysit Ghost and Jenna's kids for the time they'd be gone.

"I bet Ghost is gonna be one relaxed motherfucker, after five straight days getting shitloads of tail," Gunner says, giving me a wolfish grin.

"Not sure how they could pack much more in than they already do," I chuckle.

Ghost and Jenna are all over each other most of the time. Even with two young kids, they still act like teenagers around each other. Which is fitting, because they *had* been teenagers when they first got together. Ghost told me the whole story one night, when we happened to be sitting outside the bar having a smoke. He and Jenna had a short fling one summer when she'd been home trying to get her shit together after a rough semester at college. After they hooked up, Jenna left town again, and there'd been a span of about five years where Ghost didn't see her at all. When she came back to Tanner Springs, she had a little boy named Noah in tow. It didn't take long for Ghost and Jenna to start back up again in secret. Eventually, it came out that they had gotten back together — and that Ghost was Noah's daddy.

It's amazing how things work out sometimes, I think to myself. All that time, Ghost and Jenna were apart, living their own lives. And now here they are: sure enough of what they have together to tie the knot and settle down as a family.

I can't imagine it, personally. I can't imagine trusting a woman enough to believe in something permanent like that. Granted, Jenna is about as solid as they come. Hell, I completely understand why Ghost wanted to stand up in front of his friends and family and make it official with her. If I had someone I was that sure about, maybe I'd feel the same way. But in my experience, women like Jenna are pretty damn rare. And the crazy ones are a dime a dozen.

A sour taste rises up in my throat, and I snort in disgust. I grab my beer and take a long pull to wash the taste away. I try not to think about shit I can't change. Doesn't do any good anyway.

Just then, the door to the clubhouse opens, and Tweak comes sauntering in. He lifts his chin at us in greeting but doesn't stop on his way to the back of the clubhouse. Gunner lifts his hand in a wave then turns to me, his eyes twinkling. "I still don't think Tweak's quite forgiven us for putting his bike up in that tree," he murmurs, laughter in his voice.

I can't help but grin at the memory. "Can't say I completely blame him," I answer. Getting Tweak's bike back down from the tree had been a little trickier than we had expected. Turned out, the bike shifted in the branches and got stuck as hell. Tweak and four of the other guys ended up having to take a chain saw up there and saw off one of them, and the bike almost fell out of the tree and came crashing to the ground. The brothers' little drunken prank had almost cost Tweak his prized Road King, and he wasn't quite ready to forget it just yet.

"He'll get over it eventually. Hell, no harm no foul, right? Except for Geno's tree, of course." It was true, Geno wasn't exactly happy about the damage we'd done either.

Gunner shakes his head and grins at me. "God *damn*, Ghost's wedding was one hell of a party. We haven't had one like that in quite a while."

"No shit, brother," I say, clapping him on the back.

Gunner gets up to take a leak, and I sit there and finish my beer. It *was* a hell of a good time, I think as I smile to myself.

Even though my favorite memory of the evening has more to do with the hot photographer. Samantha.

I really, *really* need to get her out of my mind.

Not long after Gunner comes back from taking a piss, Ghost comes walking through the front door of the clubhouse. The brothers crowd around him, welcoming him home and slapping him on the back.

"Well, Ghost, what's it like banging a married chick?" Brick jokes as the others laugh.

"Watch it, brother," Angel warns him. "That's my sister you're talking about."

"Okay, okay, sorry," Brick corrects himself. "What's it like banging Angel's married sister?"

Angel pulls back a fist and pretends he's gonna slug Brick, who ducks and starts cracking up.

"Aren't you glad to be back here with the lot of these gobshites?" Thorn sighs, shaking his head.

"I haven't missed it nearly as much as you'd think," Ghost grins.

Tank rolls his eyes. "You love us. You were crying into your beer every night thinking about us while you were gone."

"Brother, I was *way* too busy for that," Ghost tells him. "Although, I *was* wondering, did Tweak ever get his bike out of Geno's tree?"

Just then Rock emerges from the back. "So this is what all the noise is about out here," he growls. He nods toward Ghost. "Good to see you, brother," he says gruffly. "Wife doin' okay?"

Ghost smirks. "She's doing great, thanks."

"Good deal." Rock turns to the rest of us. "Put the welcome wagon on hold. Church in three."

"Well, there it is. Honeymoon officially over," Ghost mutters with a grin.

We file into the chapel and take our normal seats around the table. Rock comes in last, and sits down heavily at the head place.

"Calling this meeting to order," Rock bellows, striking the gavel on the table. "Glad you're back, Ghost. We've got a lot to talk about."

Chapter 6

SAMANTHA

I raise my arms in a long, painful stretch and wince at a sudden twinge. My back is *killing* me.

I've been sitting at my workspace for close to four hours, editing photos of Jenna and Cas's wedding and compiling them into an online wedding gallery. I should really take a break, but I want to finish putting together the perfect collection of shots for her, and I have a ton to choose from.

One of the most important aspects of doing wedding photography is creating a gallery — and eventually a wedding album — that really captures the mood and the atmosphere of the couple's big day. You might think that would be easy, or that most weddings are basically the same in that regard. But in fact, every wedding has its own story to tell. And it's my job to bring that unique story out through the photos.

Sometimes, telling that story involves selectively... *muting* certain parts of it. Like the wedding I did a few months ago, where the mother of the bride showed up in a white dress that rivaled the bride's wedding gown in splendor. The mom was a plastic surgery disaster with enough makeup on to make Arnold Schwarzenegger look like Angelina Jolie. The bride's parents were divorced, and her dad was remarried to a much younger woman. It was pretty clear the bride's mom was having a serious midlife freakout, trying to compete with both her ex-husband's new wife and her own daughter. Understandably, the bride had a complete meltdown while we were doing the pre-wedding photo shoot of the families.

Yeah, try putting together pictures of *that* wedding that won't just remind the bride of how horrible her mom was on her big day. It was a challenge, to say the least.

Luckily, in the case of Jenna and Cas — or Ghost, as his fellow motorcycle club members call him — I don't have to do any selective editing. The bride was radiant, the groom was handsome, and everyone had an absolutely great time. And since I made sure not to take pictures of anything X-rated at the reception, most of the shots I snapped are usable. It's just a question of selecting the best ones to tell the story of the day.

When I finally think I have everything edited and in place the way I want it, I stand up, take a walk around the carriage house, and then grab my laptop and take it over to the couch. It's time to look at the whole thing like I'm seeing it for the first time — as though I'm Jenna and Cas. What will *they* see when they open up the gallery and start to click through?

I've set up the gallery in roughly chronological order. So the first images show establishing shots of the farm, a few of the guests laughing and talking, and some photos of Cas pre-wedding, holding Mariana and looking happy. Then there are a few pictures of the guests gathering around the spot where Cas and Jenna will be saying their vows.

And then, my heart jumps in my chest as a closeup of Hawk flashes up on the screen, bent over his guitar.

I've been working on these pictures for a few days now, and since the only photos of Hawk I took were from the beginning of the ceremony, I haven't seen these in a while. In spite of myself, my stomach does a little flip as I study his chiseled features. The strong jaw. The sensual lips. The shadow of a beard. His dirty blond hair falls over his eyes as he plays. My breathing speeds up just a bit.

I click to the next pictures, a collage of his hands as he plays. I've always had a weird thing about hands. They're one of the first things I look at on a guy. I can't explain exactly what it is about some hands that I find attractive, but it's not something I can turn on or off. You could show me the handsomest guy on the planet, and if I don't like his hands, he'll leave me totally cold.

Hawk's hands are square and strong. Masculine. They look like hands that can *do* things, *fix* things. I gaze at the photo collage, at the way his fingers play over the frets and strum the strings. These are hands that know how to be subtle. Not just how to hammer, but to stroke.

I click through a couple more pictures of Hawk. My skin is starting to feel electric. I keep thinking about his hands. Wondering what it would feel like to have them on me: touching me, caressing me. Dimly, I'm aware that maybe I've put too many pictures of him at the beginning of the gallery. *Maybe I should take a few of them out...*

And then, the photo that makes me stop in my tracks, and draw in a sharp breath.

The one where he's looking straight at the camera — straight at *me* — a teasing half-smile playing on his lips.

Oh, my gosh...

A shiver runs through me. His hazel eyes are slightly mocking, a challenge in his expression. Before I can push the memory away, I hear his low growl in my ear when I asked him if Hawk was his real name.

"Real enough. Besides, you'll like it a lot better when you're screaming it with my head between your legs."

I stare now at his eyes, transfixed, my nipples growing taut. A low ache begins between my legs. For a second, I look away, embarrassed — as though he can see me staring at him. Then, unable to help myself, I drag my eyes back to the photo. I trace the outline of his lips on the screen. My skin prickles as I remember how it felt to be in his arms — how tightly he held me against him when I fell off the speaker...

A sharp rap on the door of the carriage house jolts me from my thoughts, making me jump.

"Jesus!" I hiss, slamming the laptop shut like I've been caught doing something bad. I go to the door and look out. It's Lourdes, my grandmother's housekeeper.

"Your grandmother wants to see you in the main house," Lourdes informs me when I open the door.

"Okay," I nod, and glance back toward my computer. "Let her know I'll be there in a few minutes. I just have to finish something up."

Lourdes presses her lips together and tries to keep her face devoid of expression. "Your grandmother says now," she says simply.

I suppress a groan. I don't know why my grandmother can't just call me or text me like a normal person, instead of using Lourdes to *summon* me. It's embarrassing, and it's not Lourdes's job.

Irritation flares up inside me, but I try to push it down. This isn't Lourdes's fault, after all, and I don't want to take it out on her. "Okay," I sigh. "I'll be right there."

Lourdes nods once, then turns back toward the main house.

I shut the door and shake my head, my eyes rolling practically out of my head. Of course Gram said she needs to see me *now*. Even though in all likelihood, she's just going to ask me to take her poodle Mary Jane out for a walk or something. Other people wait for Gram, but Gram waits for no one.

I'm still flustered and uncomfortably warm from looking at the pictures of Hawk on my laptop when I wander into my bedroom to put on something more presentable than the tank top and faded leggings I'm wearing. I know Lourdes couldn't have known what I was doing — or at least, what I was *thinking* about doing. But all the same, I'm embarrassed to be caught having thoughts like that. Especially about someone I have no business thinking about in that way.

When I reach the bedroom, I slip off the tank, grab a bra from the dresser drawer, and find a button-down shirt in my closet. Kicking off my leggings, I find a pair of jeans that aren't too wrinkled and put them on instead. I pull the elastic band out of my hair, run a brush through it, and give myself a quick glance in the dresser mirror. *Good enough.* It's not much, but at least maybe my clean-up won't invite a full-on critique of my wardrobe from Gram. She has very definite opinions about what is and isn't appropriate to wear in front of other people.

After slipping on a pair of ballet flats, I walk back out into the main room, out the front door, and across the backyard to the main house as I wonder what she wants to talk to me about.

Chapter 7

SAMANTHA

My grandmother, Phyllis Jennings, is one of the upstanding members of the citizenry of Tanner Springs. Her husband — my father's father — was a prominent banker in town. I never knew Grandpa Jennings. He died many years ago, when I was a child. And frankly, I didn't know Gram growing up, either. My dad skipped town on my mom when I was a baby, and apart from a few grainy photos, I barely even knew what he looked like.

I met Gram right after my mother died of cancer, when I was nineteen. I barely knew of her existence, but I guess she had known of mine. Given that she didn't know my dad's whereabouts either, I counted as basically the only remaining direct family she had, apart from a sister-in-law who lived about an hour away. A few weeks after my mother's funeral, Gram sent me a letter asking me to come visit her in Tanner Springs. We had an awkward but not entirely unpleasant first meeting, at the end of which she silently pressed an envelope into my hands that ended up containing several hundred dollars.

After that, we kept in formal and infrequent touch, mostly through cards and letters at holidays. About two years ago, Gram's letters started coming more frequently. She told me her health was starting to fail, and eventually asked me if I would move to Tanner Springs, to keep her company in her last months. She had a fully furnished carriage house, she said, and it was mine to stay in for as long as I liked.

It just so happened that Gram's request couldn't have come at a better time. I was just pulling myself together after a breakup with the man who would completely sour me on the idea of marriage, and the prospect of getting out of town was an appealing one. I packed up the few possessions I cared to take with me into my little car and drove five hours south to Tanner Springs, expecting to find a frail, dying shadow of the grandmother I knew. Instead, she was as hale and hearty as ever — apart from a recent acquisition of hearing aids, which she despised and swore she didn't need.

I probably should have been angry that my grandmother basically tricked me into moving to Tanner Springs. But frankly, it's not like I had left that much of a life back in the city. So, in exchange for eating a few meals with her per week and listening to her complain about whatever's pissing her off on any given day, I have a place to stay I could never afford on my own and the flexibility to build up my photography business.

When I find Gram in the main house, she's standing at the large front window to the sitting room. She's staring outside with a sour expression on her face. Her aging poodle, Mary Jane, is by her side, watching the goings-on with much the same expression.

"Those neighbors across the street have a tree service over there," she sniffs disdainfully. "They're going to pull down that beautiful old oak tree in their front yard. I just know it." She shakes her head as if she can't believe their audacity. "That tree has been there forever. It's part of the neighborhood."

My gaze follows hers. "It's also taller than their house, and it's leaning," I remark. "One good storm and that thing would crash through their roof."

Gram purses her lips. She doesn't like to be contradicted. "Well, there must be *something* they can do," she says stubbornly. Beside her, Mary Jane emits a low growl of agreement. "One doesn't just tear down a tree like that on a *whim*." The corners of her mouth turn down. "That tree's been here much longer than *they* have."

A small smile lifts the edges of my mouth. So *that's* the problem. The neighbors across the street, the Cantwells, are a young professional couple who moved in a couple of months ago with their two twin boys. He's a veterinarian and she's a realtor, if I remember correctly. The house used to be owned by the former mayor of Tanner Springs, who left town a while ago under somewhat mysterious circumstances. Gram herself doesn't know exactly what happened to him. It's clear from the way she talks, though, that she enjoyed the prestige of living across the street from the mayor. I don't think the new neighbors, with their two rambunctious sons, quite live up to her standards.

"You can't just tear down a piece of history in a neighborhood like this," Gram is muttering to herself. I know better than to argue with her, so I try to do the next best thing.

"Gram," I interrupt her, changing the subject, "Lourdes said you wanted to see me?"

"Oh. Yes." Reluctantly, Gram turns away from the window and faces me. "I got you a job," she says with a satisfied nod.

I suppress a groan. This is exactly what I was worried about. Ever since I got to town five months ago, Gram has been trying to convince me that photography isn't a *real* job, and that I need something more respectable, more steady. It doesn't matter how many times I've told her I'm getting a decent amount of work and don't need any help from her connections. She is convinced that I'm wasting my time and energy on a career that will never pan out.

"Gram," I begin, trying to keep the irritation out of my voice. "I really appreciate your concern, but I told you, I'm working on building up my photography business. I can't take on any…"

"Oh, nonsense, Samantha." Gram cuts me off impatiently. "I'm sure you'll have plenty of time in between working to take your little photographs."

My blood starts to heat up at the reference to my "little" photographs. It's not news that Gram doesn't think much of what I do, but it's still amazing how quickly she can get under my skin with remarks like this. I start to repeat the mantra in my mind that I use whenever she's making me crazy: *She's an old woman, she's set in her ways, she doesn't have any family except you, she's just trying to help in her own way…*

"My good friend RuthEllen Hanson is director of the library," Gram continues, raising her chin. "She's looking for someone to work there, perhaps part-time to start, and then eventually full-time." Gram looks at me and gives me a thin smile. "Of course, when I told her my granddaughter would be available, she was immediately interested in hiring you."

"But Gram," I sigh, trying a different tack this time. "Wouldn't it be better if, you know, I actually *applied* for positions I actually *wanted*?"

"Well, I can't imagine why you wouldn't want this position. It's certainly not particularly *challenging*. Even someone with no education can do it," she says pointedly, referring to the fact that I decided to skip college. "All you'll be doing is checking out books and re-shelving things. How hard can it be? All you need to know is the alphabet." She flashes me a look as though she can't believe I'm looking her gift horse in the mouth.

I push down the urge to argue with her. "I'm sure it's a lovely job," I say instead. "And thank you for thinking of me. But I just think…"

"What?" she interrupts, her tone challenging.

Oh, God… She is just not going to let this go, I know. It's really no use trying to fight her on this. And if I turn down this job, she'll just look for another one for me. I take a deep breath and let it out.

"Okay, Gram," I say wearily. "I'll contact your friend…"

"RuthEllen," she says promptly.

"RuthEllen. I'll contact her for an interview." *Maybe RuthEllen will hate me, and Gram will be satisfied that at least I tried,* I tell myself, but I know better. My grandmother is one of the stubbornest people I know, and she won't rest until I have what she considers a "decent" job.

"Excellent, dear," she says in a dismissive tone, but she seems pleased. She turns her attention back to the front window, and I understand I'm being dismissed.

"Oh, and one more thing, Samantha," she calls after me as I turn to go.

"Yes?" I ask, glancing back.

"Please take Mary Jane for a walk."

Chapter 8
HAWK

"I happened to run into Len Baker this morning," Rock is saying. "He happened to ask me how the permitting process for the warehouse is going."

"'*Happened* to run into'?" Brick comments sardonically, noting Rock's repetition of the word. Len Baker is the chief of police for the city of Tanner Springs.

"Yeah," grunts Rock. "He told me he thinks his days are numbered as police chief. Holloway's looking to replace him, rumor has it." Rock takes a long look around the table. "He said Holloway's working pretty hard behind the scenes to get his preferred candidate for county sheriff elected, too."

The men grow silent for a moment, taking in his words. There's no way this is good news for us. Of course, we should have seen it coming. The new mayor, Jarred Holloway, has been crowing about cleaning up the "crime element" in Tanner Springs. And by crime element, it seems pretty clear he means the Lords of Carnage MC.

The warehouse Rock mentioned talking to Len Baker about is one we own on the south side of town. It's where we keep inventory of various kinds. Including some that's less than legal. Mainly, guns.

Lately, though, shit's been heating up enough that the club's been looking to get out of the gun running business. We've been tossing around the idea of a new project: to renovate the warehouse and make it into a garage and repair shop. Most of us have a decent amount of experience fixing engines of various types. So far, though, we haven't made any moves on that front.

It looks like that may be about to change.

Gun running used to be one of our club's largest sources of income. Tanner Springs is situated along what the Feds call the "Iron Pipeline." The Pipeline is the route along Interstate 95 and its connector highways. It's the main route for gun smuggling between a bunch of the southern states and states up north in New England that have stricter gun laws.

Most of the guns we run end up in New York City and New Jersey — especially to places with a lot of gang activity like the Bronx and Chinatown. Demand is steady, prices are good, and the Lords have solid connections and a lock on the gun smuggling traffic in this part of the state. For a long time, it kept us sitting pretty, financially speaking. And in spite of the risks, it was more than worth it for us — in part because of a long-standing arrangement we had with Abe Abbott.

Abe Abbott was the mayor of Tanner Springs until about two years ago. He also happened to be the father of our club's Vice President, Angel. The arrangement between the Lords and Abe Abbott didn't actually have anything to do with Angel being his son, though. This was a deal that Rock cut with Abe a long time ago, back when Abe was first running for mayor.

The deal went something like this: the Lords did what needed to be done to keep the crime rate down low in Tanner Springs, including keeping bad shit from outside from coming into town. In exchange, Mayor Abbott and the TSPD looked the other way on a lot of the Lords' questionable activity, as long as that activity was kept out of the public eye.

It was an arrangement that worked well for both sides for many years. Abbott kept getting re-elected, and the Lords kept on with business as usual. We even do some fundraisers in the community, to keep the fine upstanding citizens of Tanner Springs from clutching their pearls whenever they see us ride by.

Well, that shit all came to an end a little over a year ago. After Abe Abbott disappeared, and the deputy mayor lost the election campaign to Jarred Fucking Holloway.

For years — as far back as I can remember — Mayor Abbott never had a serious challenger for his re-election campaigns. But a couple of years ago, Abe found himself up against it in the last election cycle, facing a young upstart on a mission to make Tanner Springs his own little empire.

Jarred Holloway grew up here in Tanner Springs, the son of an asshole lawyer who always thought he was better than everybody else in town. Even as a kid, Jarred Holloway was a snot-nosed son of a bitch — the kind of kid that would tell other kids in his class that his dad would sue them if they didn't let him have his way. He was four years ahead of me in school, and damned if the best memory I have of him isn't when a group of guys pulled him into a corner after school one day and beat the shit out of him for telling the principal they were smoking weed in one of the bathrooms.

Holloway went away to the state university, and came back to town years later with an MBA and an even bigger attitude than he had before he left. Without ever having held a public office before, he launched himself into the mayoral campaign, using his family money and connections to raise a big pot of campaign cash before Abe Abbott even knew what was happening.

At first, it seemed like Holloway was just doing it to make a name for himself as an important player in town. After all, Abe was well liked, and Tanner Springs was prospering. Crime was low, the streets were well-maintained, repairs were quick whenever a sewer main or something went out. He even managed to sort of buck the trend of decaying small towns, getting some new commercial developments going up around town. It seemed pretty unlikely a young upstart with no track record could unseat a popular and successful mayor with years of experience.

So, like a lot of other people, Abe Abbott didn't take Holloway seriously for quite a while. But what he didn't account for was that Holloway had figured out something important. Since Holloway didn't have any experience at all, and was up against a strong candidate who *did*, he chose the only strategy that could have worked for him:

He attacked Abbott on his *strengths* to make them look like weaknesses.

Holloway started making appearances at the Rotary Club and sending out flyers with one relentless message: There's a crime problem in Tanner Springs. He said it in every single speech, in every single appearance he made, and in every single editorial he sent to the local paper. It didn't matter that it wasn't true. Because after a while — after people had heard it over and over and over again — some of them started to believe it.

And from there, it wasn't hard for him to start directly connecting the "crime problem" to the standing mayor, Abe Abbott. And to the one visible "dangerous" group in the city: The Lords of Carnage.

Shit started heating up for Abe. He started to get desperate for "wins" to show the community that he was still their best bet as mayor. Unfortunately, desperation leads people to make some *really* bad fucking decisions, and Abe was no different. In a last-ditch attempt to get financing for a development he was working on, Abe Abbott made the biggest mistake of his life.

He went to our rival MC, the Iron Spiders, for the money.

Of course, the Lords didn't know that. Abe would never have told us. But when the debt he owed to the Spiders started dragging him in further than he could handle, he came to our club and asked for a loan. The Lords turned him down, and in desperation, Abe went back to the Spiders and offered to sell them information on us as another way to pay them back.

When everything came to light about his double-dealing, Abe ended up with both the Iron Spiders and the Lords looking to settle the score with him. Abe disappeared. Most likely, the Spiders got to him. Which might have been a mercy. Because if they hadn't, the Lords would have had to decide whether to end the man who was not only the mayor of Tanner Springs, but also the father of our VP, and the father-in-law of our Sergeant at Arms.

After Abe Abbott disappeared, the deputy mayor, Duncan Mummer, took over running the town. He even put in his bid to run for Abbott's seat. But Mummer is a bumbling, forgettable guy with an intermittent stammer, and he was no match for Holloway's freight train approach. Holloway won the election with over seventy percent of the votes.

And ever since, the Lords of Carnage have been in his sights.

"What do you mean, Baker was asking about the permit?" I ask Rock now, confused. "We haven't applied for one."

"Yeah," Rock mutters. "I think he knew that. I think he was trying to give us a warning." He shifts in his chair. "Like, maybe he's saying we need to move on that shit, ASAP. Len's one of the few people of Abbott's left that Holloway hasn't replaced with one of his cronies." His eyes turn dark. "He's one of the few people we still have on the inside. And not for much longer, sounds like."

"You think he's trying to tell us someone could go sniffing around the warehouse sometime soon?" Brick asks, his face turning dark and angry.

"Yeah. Yeah, I do," Rock nods. "I don't want to take any chances. Time's a-wastin'. We need to get those guns gone, now. All of 'em."

"How we gonna do that?" Tweak asks.

"Talk to the Death Devils," I say immediately. I've been thinking about this for a while. The Devils are an MC to the east of us. We've never had any sort of partnership with them before, but we haven't had any trouble with them, either. Their president, Ozzy, is grizzly as fuck, but his men respect him. And we know they used to run guns around Iron Spiders territory to the south.

"Yeah," agrees Tank, nodding toward me. "They're the best bet of unloading everything right away."

Angel speaks up. "Hell, we should have seen this coming," he says grimly. "We probably should have approached the Devils with this months ago. It gets that shit gone, plus forming an alliance with them is the best defense against the Spiders." The Iron Spiders have been trying to push north into our territory for a while now. It's been getting tougher and tougher to beat them back.

Rock turns his head and looks at Angel sharply. He's quick to see statements like this as a challenge to his authority.

"Is that right?" he says, his voice going cold as steel. "Then why didn't you suggest it? *Months* ago?"

Beside me, Gunner gives a low whistle, quiet enough that only I can hear him.

There's been a weird tension building for a while between Rock and Angel. You don't see it very often, but it surfaces every once in a while, like now. It's not great to see. Between a prez and a VP, there needs to be absolute trust for an MC to function well. Gunner said to me a couple weeks ago he thinks Rock holds it against Angel that Abe Abbott betrayed the club, because Abe is Angel's father. That seems pretty fucked up to me, though. After all, Rock's the one who struck the deal with Abe in the first place, all those years ago. The club wouldn't have had any relationship to Abbott at all if it hadn't been for that.

"Well, whenever we *should* have done it, let's do it now," Ghost cuts in. "If Len was giving us a heads up, we need those guns out of the warehouse *yesterday*. Before Holloway's men come looking."

On the other side of the table, Striker shakes his head. "Fuck. This shit sure was easier when Abbott was mayor."

No one says anything for a moment.

"Never thought I'd be sorry to see that fucking traitor gone," Rock mutters angrily. "But there are days."

I glance over at Angel, but his expression doesn't change.

"Okay," Rock says finally. His hand comes down on the table with a loud slap. "Let's vote on this. All in favor of approaching the Death Devils about taking our remaining stock of guns off our hands."

It's unanimous. Rock tells Angel, Ghost, and Geno to be ready to head to Devils territory to meet with Ozzy and his men. Then he bangs the gavel, and the rest of us head out to the bar, to wait for what happens next.

Chapter 9

SAMANTHA

"No, please, if you could just —!"

For the fourth time this morning, I've been hung up on. This officially exhausts my list of every plumber in Tanner Springs I could find online. Every one I've called says they're booked up and unavailable as soon as I give them Gram's name.

Gram gave me the task of finding a handyman to fix a leak under the kitchen sink that Lourdes found yesterday. Thankfully, it's not exactly an emergency, but the bucket that's sitting under the pipe needs to be emptied every few hours, and it seems to be getting worse. Frowning in frustration, I go back online and try to find listings of any other people in town to call, but no luck.

I sit at Gram's kitchen table, unsure what to do next. I can't really go upstairs and tell her I'm striking out at finding someone. She'll just tell me to keep trying and send me back down here. And poor Lourdes can't really use the sink until it gets fixed.

Finally, in desperation, I go into the sitting room, find the YouTube app on my phone and start searching for "how to fix a leaky pipe." I spend about fifteen minutes looking through videos, and wondering if there's any way I can manage to do this myself without causing a real emergency. I finally find one that seems to give good step by step instructions, and watch it all the way through. I take note of the tools I'll need, pushing down the little voice in my head that keeps piping up and saying, *Are you crazy? This is going to turn into a scenario you'll look back on and ask yourself what you were thinking.*

No, I tell her. *I can do this.*

Well, at least I can try.

I go back into the kitchen, take a bunch of pictures of the pipes, and head off to the hardware store, muttering a pep talk to myself the whole way in the car.

When I walk into Sunderland's Hardware, there are already four or five customers being assisted by the people working there. It looks like there won't be anyone available to help me for a few minutes. Uncertainly, I peer up at the signs at the ends of the aisles, and walk back through the store until I find the one labeled "Plumbing Supplies."

I'm concentrating so hard that I don't even see the mountain of flesh until I quite literally run smack into it.

"Oooff," I grunt as my face smashes into a broad, muscular chest.

"Steady," a deep voice says, two large, strong hands grabbing me by the arms. Beside us, something falls to the floor.

"I'm so sorry!" I gasp. I stagger a little and finally regain my balance. The hands are still holding me by the upper arms. My face flushes hot with embarrassment, and I raise my eyes to look at the man, who must think I'm a complete idiot.

My brain registers a black leather vest. Patches decorate the chest on both sides.

A square, strong jaw with the hint of a beard. Skin tanned a golden brown.

Sensual lips curved into an amused smirk.

Oh, shit.

"Huh," Hawk rumbles, a mocking laugh in his voice. "Of all the places to run into the wedding photographer." He takes his hands off my arms and crosses them in front of his chest.

Humiliation instantly starts to transform into indignation. "What's that supposed to mean?" I ask hotly.

He shrugs. "Nothing. You just don't seem like the kind of girl who hangs out at hardware stores."

"What, just because I'm a woman means I don't know anything about hardware stuff?" I demand. Then I remember that I *don't* actually have any idea what I'm doing.

"I didn't say that," he chuckles softly. "I know plenty of women who know how to use a wrench."

I'm only slightly mollified. "Well, okay, then," I huff.

"So, what's the project?"

"What?" My face starts to flush.

"What's the project you're getting supplies for?" His tone is indulgent, and it infuriates me. Somehow, I just know he can *tell* I don't know what I'm doing. It makes me want to smack that smug smile off his face.

Hating that I've let myself be backed into a corner, I consider lying to him. Then I realize I don't even know enough about repairing things to concoct a convincing lie. I toss my head defiantly. "I'm fixing a leaky pipe under my gram's kitchen sink," I say, trying to sound like this is something I do all the time.

Hawk lets out a low whistle. "I'm impressed. You actually know how to do that?"

Ugh. Can this conversation just be *over* now? "Not exactly," I admit, a challenge in my voice. "But I found some videos online about how to do it."

"I see. Videos." He nods seriously. "Very instructive."

I know he's teasing me. I shouldn't let him get to me. But since I'm already worried that maybe I can't do this, the fact that he doesn't seem to think I can either makes my brain start telling me that this is all a fool's errand, and that I should just give up now.

A wave of uncertainty rises up inside me as I glance around the store. All the employees are still talking to other customers. I look back up at Hawk, who's still standing there with his arms crossed and that damn cocky smirk on his face.

Hawk's probably the kind of guy who knows how to fix things. I bet he knows all about how to fix a leaky kitchen sink.

Am I really going to screw this up? Is it really stupid that I'm even trying?

"It can't be *that* hard… can it?" I ask him in a small voice.

As soon as the words are out of my mouth, I regret them. I don't know why I just gave him an opening to keep making fun of me.

But instead of doing that, he surprises me by taking my question seriously.

"No. It's not that hard," he concedes, nodding slightly. "Unless something goes wrong, that is." Hawk cocks his head at me and frowns. "Why don't you just call in a plumber?"

"I tried," I admit. Frustration creeps into my voice, and in spite of myself, I feel my guard slipping a little. "But everyone I've called says they're booked up." I sigh. "Handymen hate my grandmother. I literally think they've all banded together and taken a vow not to do jobs for her anymore."

Hawk smirks. "Oh, come on. How bad could she be?"

I eye him. "You don't know my grandmother, do you? Phyllis Jennings?"

He splutters, laughing. "Oh, Jesus. Phyllis *Jennings* is your grandmother?"

"Yeah," I nod wryly. "So you see what I mean."

"I do." He continues to snicker for a moment, and then something in his face changes.

Hawk bends down then, and pick a small, flat square up off the floor. It's a packet of sandpaper. He must have dropped it when I ran into him, I realize, remembering that something fell.

"Well, then," he says, drawing himself up to his full height. "Tell you what. Let's grab what we need, and I'll come over and take a look at it for you."

In the "I'm a strong woman who doesn't need help from any man" version of this story, I tell Hawk to go to hell. Then I go back to Gram's and fix the leak myself.

This isn't that version of the story.

I take a deep breath and let it out. "You really don't need to do that," I say, shaking my head.

"I know that," he rumbles, giving me a cocky smirk that makes my heart speed up just a little. "I don't do shit I don't want to do." He turns down the plumbing aisle. "Come on," he says, not looking back. "Tell me what's going on with the leak so I know what we're looking at."

As we stand in the aisle, Hawk asks me what exactly the problem is, how bad the leak is, and where it seems to be coming from. I show him some of the pictures I took and point to where I think the water's coming from.

"Good idea to take photos," he tells me approvingly. "That was smart." I try to ignore the flush of pride I feel at his words. So at least I'm not a *complete* idiot, anyway.

"Okay," he says when I'm done explaining. "It sounds like maybe it's a leak at the valve stem. The gaskets and O rings might need to be repacked and replaced." Hawk finds some small packets and pulls them off the display, then wanders further down to the end of the aisle and picks up a small plastic jar. "Sealant," he tells me. "Just in case."

I follow Hawk to the checkout counter. Somehow, his bearing has changed, and the cocky bastard I met at Jenna and Cas's wedding has disappeared. I get out some money to pay for the supplies, but he stops me. "Don't worry about it," he tells me. "I'll get it for now. I'll swing back by here afterwards and return whatever we don't use. You can pay me later for what we end up needing."

We go out the back door toward the parking lot. Hawk's motorcycle is parked a few spaces away from my car. I start to tell him my address, but he stops me with a grin. "I know where Phyllis Jennings lives," he says. "Across the street from Abe Abbott's old house, right?"

I nod. "That's right."

"Anyway, I'll follow you." I get into my car and pull out onto the street. Hawk pulls out behind me. I drive back to Gram's, casting occasional glances in the rear view mirror. Hawk's dark blond hair shifts in the wind, his mirrored sunglasses obscuring his piercing eyes. I remember with a shiver what it felt like to be in his strong, muscled arms.

In my chest, my heart pounds just a little harder.

Chapter 10

SAMANTHA

Gram isn't home when we get back, thankfully. She's gone to some meeting for a flower show she helps organize. I'm pretty sure she might have something to say about having a man who looks like Hawk in her house. I pray he manages to get the sink fixed and leaves before she gets back.

But although Gram's not around, Lourdes is. As Hawk and I walk in the front door, she's coming down the stairs, a dust rag in her hand. I brace myself for her questions and try to act natural.

"Hi, Lourdes," I say. "This is Hawk. He's, uh, come to fix the sink."

I'm worried this exchange might be a little awkward. After all, Hawk is hardly dressed like a plumber. But to my surprise, the exact opposite happens.

"Hey, Lulu!" Hawk says to Lourdes. "¿Así que trabajas para la bruja?"

Lourdes erupts into loud laughter. "Hawk, ¿qué haces aquí, amigo?"

And then, before I know what's happening, the two of them are conversing back and forth in rapid-fire Spanish.

I listen to the two of them for a few seconds, and just manage not to let my jaw drop on the floor that Hawk can speak another language. Finally, Hawk says something that makes Lourdes giggle like a schoolgirl and mock-slap at his shoulder.

"Hawk will fix the sink, no problem," she says to me with a wide smile. "But you keep him out of my refrigerator. He'll eat us out of house and home."

"Lulu," Hawk frowns, pretending to be hurt. "You wound me."

"It's good to see you, Hawk," she grins. "It's been a long time. Help yourself to coffee."

"Will do," he nods. We watch as she retreats toward the back of the house.

"Wow. How do you know Spanish?" I ask Hawk as I point him toward the kitchen.

He shrugs. "My parents got divorced when I was a little kid. My dad moved to Mexico. My brother and I spent summers there until he turned eighteen." He takes off his leather vest and sets it on the counter.

"You have a brother?"

"Had," he says flatly.

Oh.

I don't say anything for a few seconds. Hawk kneels down and opens the cupboard doors under the sink. Wordlessly, he starts handing me bottles of soap and boxes of trash bags. I take them, helping him clear everything out so he has space to work.

When there's nothing left underneath the sink, he gets on all fours and leans in. "No jokes about plumber's ass," he says, his tone mock-serious.

"I wouldn't dream of it," I say. I'm relieved that the tension from a few seconds ago seems to be gone. Luckily, Hawk *definitely* does not have plumber's butt. He does have… quite a *nice* butt, though. I stand awkwardly behind him as he works, trying not to notice just *how* nice it is. Unfortunately, having him there with his back to me gives me plenty of time to really get a good look at his sculpted, powerful body. He reaches toward the sink with one arm, and his gray T-shirt rides up just a bit, exposing a line of tanned skin at his waist. Even with just that little bit exposed, I can easily see how muscled his back is. A flash of color gives me just a glimpse of intricate tattoos on his torso. I find myself wondering what they look like. Whether they ripple with his muscles when he moves.

Whether they follow the curves of his tapered waist.

How far down the tattoos go.

What it would feel like to touch his hard abs, and slide my fingers against the heat of his skin…

"So, you live here with your grandma?" Hawk asks, his voice echoing slightly under the sink.

With a jolt, my traitorous mind registers that he just asked me a question.

"Um, yes. Well, in the carriage house behind the main house." I point out the kitchen window, even though he can't see me. "I've been here for almost six months now."

"That explains why I never saw you before Ghost and Jenna's wedding," he observes. "You sticking around for good?"

"I don't know," I say. "At first I was just here temporarily, but I'm doing pretty well with my photography here, so I might stay for a while and see how it goes."

Hawk doesn't say anything in reply. For a few moments, there's silence between us.

"So, how do you know Lourdes?" I ask then, a little too brightly. My voice comes out slightly strangled-sounding, but Hawk doesn't seem to notice.

"Her dad and my dad were good friends when I was a little kid," he tells me. "Before Dad moved away. And her younger sister was in my grade at school." He pulls himself out of the opening and looks at his hand, which is slightly wet. "I think her parents were sort of hoping that Lulu's sister and I would end up together, for a while."

"Oh."

So, Lourdes's sister dated Hawk in high school? Or maybe her parents just *wanted* them to date? Ridiculously, I find myself hoping it's the latter. *For God's sake, Sam, you can't be jealous. Don't be an idiot.*

And I'm not jealous. Not *really*, I mean. But after all, you'd have to be blind not to see how um, *attractive* Hawk is. I'm sure he doesn't have any trouble getting attention from women. *It's probably what makes him so damn cocky,* I think crossly.

So yeah, I'm not *jealous*. Just maybe a little *irritated* that he probably has the same mesmerizing effect on most women that he seems to be having on me.

It's not fair, really.

Suppressing a frustrated sigh, I try to pull myself back and just appreciate his beauty objectively. Like a sculpture, or something.

A *hot* sculpture.

"It looks like this is a pretty easy fix," Hawk says, interrupting my thoughts. He pulls himself out of the space and looks at me. "I just need to shut off the water and replace the gasket."

Hawk finds the valve to shut off the water, and I show him out to the garage where the tools are kept. He chooses what he needs and we come back into the kitchen. Part of me wants to ask him to show me what he's doing: it pisses me off that I don't know how to do something as useful as this. But the thought of being that close to him makes me nervous, so I don't.

I let him work for a while in silence, admiring the way the muscles in his arms flex as he wields the wrench.

"Thank you for doing this," I say lamely.

"No problem," he says, glancing up at me. "I told you, I don't do things I don't want to do."

A few more moments pass.

"Can I ask you a question?"

"Shoot."

"What's your real name?"

"Kaden. McCullough."

I turn the sounds over in my mind.

"Why do they call you Hawk, then?"

He stops what he's doing for a moment and looks at me. His eyes are dark, unreadable. "Hawks are predators," he says simply. " Once they have a target in sight, nothing stops them."

I swallow nervously. "Oh," I say again.

I don't know what kind of target he means. But I'm a little frightened of him right now.

And also a little turned on.

"Okay. Go turn on the water," Hawk murmurs, breaking into my thoughts. I do as I'm told, then come back into the kitchen. He runs the faucet for a minute or so, and grabs a dry towel from the counter to check whether there's still a drip.

"I think we're good," he says finally, pulling himself up and getting to his feet.

"Thanks again," I murmur as I watch him take his leather vest and pull it on over his shirt. "What do I owe you for the part?"

He snorts softly. "Nothing. It hardly cost anything." Looking down at the pile of stuff on the floor, he murmurs, "I'll help you put this back."

"No," I interrupt him. "I'll get it. You've been so helpful already. Your work is done here."

He nods. "Okay."

An awkward silence grows between us as I just stand there looking at him. I should just thank him and walk him to the front door. But I can't seem to move, or talk, with his eyes on mine. A second passes, and then another. My face flushes hot, from embarrassment or desire I'm not sure. His eyes seem to darken, and it feels like he's getting closer to me even though he hasn't moved a step. Finally, I manage to drag my eyes away from his, and turn my head toward the front door.

"Well," I begin, my voice strangely hoarse. "I guess I…"

At that moment, the sound of the side door opening off the porte-cochère cuts me off. A few seconds later, Gram's voice calls out.

"Lourdes?"

"I, uh, think she's upstairs," I call back. My eyes flicker to Hawk.

"This should be interesting," he murmurs.

Gram appears in the entryway to the kitchen. "Samantha," she begins, and then she stops short.

"Who is this person?" she says icily, staring at Hawk. Her eyes go not to his face, but to his tattoos and leather vest.

"This is, um, Hawk," I say lamely. "He just fixed the sink for us."

Gram's face is a mask of displeasure. "Why didn't you bring in one of our normal plumbers?"

Because no one wants to work for you. "No one was available. So Hawk generously offered to help us out of a bind." I give Gram a pleading look. "Wasn't that nice of him?"

Gram sniffs. "Well, I certainly hope you didn't leave him alone. I don't want to find out later that anything's missing from the house."

I'm mortified. "Oh, my God, *Gram!*"

But Hawk actually looks *amused*.

"Don't worry, Mrs. Jennings," he replies. "Your décor doesn't really match mine. There's not a lot here I can coordinate with human skulls and pentagrams."

Gram gives him a sour look, like she can't figure out if he's serious. Finally, she seems to decide that he's making fun of her.

"Please leave my house," she says simply, and turns away.

"No worries," he says easily. "You have a nice day, now."

"I'm so sorry about Gram," I babble as I follow him out. "I mean, it's not surprising that's how she reacted, but it was completely out of line."

"It's fine," he says. "It's not exactly the first time an old lady has pulled her handbag closer when she saw me walk by." We reach the front door and he pushes it open. "I'll see you," he says simply.

As he strides down the walk, I watch him go, a low ebb of something like longing in my stomach.

I turn back inside and put everything back under the sink, getting angrier by the second at my grandmother. When I'm done, I go looking for her, and eventually find her in the sitting room.

"Gram, that was so rude of you!" I fume. "He fixed the sink for free. You ought to be grateful."

"I'd be *grateful* if you didn't bring thugs into my house, Samantha," Gram scowls.

"If it wasn't for that *thug*, I would have had to fix the sink myself. Every single person I called this morning said they were booked up." I look her in the eye. "And you know what? I don't think they actually were booked up. I think they just didn't want to work for you, Gram."

Her eyes narrow in anger, but I'm not done.

"Not everyone exists to bow to your wishes, you know," I inform her. "Hawk did something legitimately nice for us.

The very least you could have done was thank him for the favor, and not insult him. You called him a thug, but he acted with more class than you did."

And then, because I'm afraid what else will come out of my mouth if I continue to stand there, I turn on my heel and walk out the back door toward the carriage house.

I go inside and slam the door, my emotions rioting inside me. I'm fuming at my grandmother and embarrassed at what Hawk must think of her. And of me.

Every time I think I've figured Hawk out — every time I think I've got his number — he does something to knock me off balance. He's infuriatingly cocky and crass. The first time I met him, he said filthy things, and seemed to *enjoy* making me angry. Even when he saved me from potentially injuring myself at Jenna's wedding, he had to ruin it by acting like a pig afterward. And then, just when he managed to get my body to respond to him even though I was trying like hell to resist him, he dropped me like I was on fire and walked away.

So why, after all that, did he volunteer to come fix Gram's kitchen sink? He took time out of his day to help me when I needed it. And what's more, it didn't even seem like he expected anything in return.

I feel like there's more to Hawk than I first thought. But damned if I can figure out what it is.

Sighing, I shake my head and resolve to put him out of my head. I'm walking into my little kitchen to get a glass of water when there's a light rap on my front door. *Oh great. Gram's sent Lourdes to bring me back for another tongue lashing.* I almost don't answer, but then realize I don't want to put Lourdes in the middle of anything by refusing to go over. Not bothering to look out the window, I turn the knob and yank the door open.

Standing on the other side is Hawk.

"I told you I'd see you," he growls, taking a step toward me.

Chapter 11

HAWK

I don't know what the fuck I'm doing here.

No, that's not true. I know exactly what I'm doing here. But I'm a fucking idiot for doing it.

Samantha's look of surprise when she opens the door should snap me out of it. I should make some excuse, like I left something inside her grandmother's house, and let her go look for it so I can get my shit together and leave.

But after an hour of being alone with Samantha, any resolve I possessed just flew out the goddamn window. It started when I offered to come over and fix her sink for her, and she bit that damn lower lip of hers as she tried to decide whether to let me. I spent the whole time in her grandmother's kitchen battling a raging hard-on and trying to act like I was just doing all this out of the goodness of my heart.

I almost even had myself convinced.

I take a step toward her. For just a second, her eyes flicker, and I think that maybe I've read her wrong — that she hasn't been sending me signals the whole damn time I've been here. But then, her lips part, just a little, and I see her chest rise as she takes in a quick, shallow breath.

Even if she doesn't know it yet, her body's waiting for me.

The hard-on I've been fighting throbs against my zipper as I take another step, crossing the threshold. She takes a small step back, but it's not to get away from me. It's to let me in.

My hand comes up to fist in her hair. Her eyes flutter, half-closing. Her head tilts back, and my mouth comes down on hers.

God. She tastes sweet. Her lips are soft and pliant, opening to mine without complaint. My tongue finds hers, and she moans into my mouth softly. Her arms twine around my neck, her body molding to mine. It's like a goddamn explosion has gone off inside me. I want everything at once — I want her every way I can think of, and I can think of a *lot* of ways.

I kick the door closed and walk her backward, one hand still in her hair and the other pulling her hard against me.

Blindly, because I've never been here before, I press her against what turns out to be a heavy dining room table. It moves slightly against our weight. I think about laying her down on it and taking her, and instantly my cock is hard as a steel pipe.

Up until now, the only thing on my mind is getting off — because even though I've been trying as hard as I can to put Samantha out of my mind for the last week, that doesn't mean I haven't jacked off thinking about her more times than I can count. But then I slide my hand up under her shirt and my thumb brushes against her nipple, and Samantha throws back her head and *moans*. And in that instant, something shifts, and all I want to do is hear that sound again. I want to hear her whisper my name. I want to hear her beg. I want to feel her shudder against me as she comes.

My mouth crashes down on hers again, devouring her, as my hand reaches behind her and undoes her bra. I push under it and graze my thumb against her nipple again, swallowing her whimper. I pinch, and my cock tightens even more when she reaches up to grip my arms. Her hips writhe against me.

I push Samantha back so she's lying on the table, her legs gripping around my waist. She moans again, angling her hips so that my hardness is pressed against her softness. She's just as turned on as I am, and I can't wait to send her over the fucking edge. Sliding her shirt up, I bend down and take one breast into my mouth, sucking and biting at the taut bud as she squirms and cries out. Her hands fly to my head, clutching at my hair. I continue to tease and suck at her, my hips bucking almost involuntarily against her hot center. I hear a crash as one of the dining room chairs topples over. Samantha's breath hitches in her throat.

A soft but persistent knock on the door threads its way through the silence after the crash.

"Shit!" Samantha hisses.

"What?" My mouth is traveling down the soft skin of her stomach toward the promised land, and I'm not about to stop now. But Samantha pushes my head away from her and scoots herself into a sitting position on the table.

"It's Lourdes," she whispers. "I know it. Gram's sent her over here to get me."

"So ignore her," I murmur, nipping at her neck.

"I can't," she protests. "You don't know Gram. She'll come over here herself if I don't go."

Samantha pulls down her shirt and runs a hand through her tousled hair to smooth it. "Hide," she orders me, and scrambles off the table to go answer the door.

I move behind a large pillar off to one side of the room, feeling like a jackass. I hear Samantha open the door, then Lulu's voice. Samantha tells her she'll be there in a minute, and the door closes again.

"I have to go," she says when she comes back to where I'm hiding. She looks at me then, like she wants to say something else, but in the end she just turns and heads out the door toward the main house.

I'm left standing in the middle of the room, my cock painfully hard, with nothing but the memory of Samantha's soft skin under my hands.

I feel like I'm emerging from a moment of temporary insanity. My mind had taken a complete leave of absence as soon as I'd decided to go back to Samantha's carriage house instead of just taking off on my bike. Standing here, it's almost like I just woke from a coma or something. I look around at the tasteful and expensive furnishings — no doubt chosen by Samantha's grandmother — and wonder what the fuck is wrong with me.

Remembering why I walked away from her at Ghost's wedding in the first place, I start for the front door. I should get out of here before Samantha gets back. This was a stupid fuck up. I should have known better than to tempt fate by agreeing to fix her grandma's goddamn sink. I'm smarter than that. Or at least I thought I was.

But as my hand goes to the knob, I hesitate. She'll be back soon, probably. And if the last few minutes are any indication, she wants me as much as I want her. My cock throbs in my jeans at the thought of what was about to happen. I know it still can. All I have to do is sit down on that overstuffed couch and wait.

But somehow, waiting seems too much like admitting — to myself and to Samantha — that she's different. She's someone I want more than just a quick lay from. And I swore to myself I wouldn't let myself get involved. Not with anyone, and least of all with someone who could end up fucking with my head.

Wanting is dangerous, I tell myself again. Turning the knob, I let myself out and shut the door behind me.

Chapter 12

HAWK

Instead of driving back to my place, I head in the direction of the clubhouse. I need some distraction right now. Hopefully in the form of some strong booze — and if I can get my head into it, some easy pussy.

But even as I think this, I know I won't be sinking my cock into one of the club girls tonight. Just the thought of it feels depressing as shit.

"Goddamnit!" I roar into the wind, my hands curling around the grips as though I could crush them. I'm sick of this fucking shit. I'm sick of being a goddamn sap. I haven't given a shit about any woman in years, and I'm not about to start now.

Furiously, I throttle the bike and blow past the clubhouse onto the open highway. I know If I go to the club right now, I won't be happy until I've picked a fight with one of the brothers and punched somebody. I need to calm down before get there.

I need to ride.

Just outside of town is one of my favorite roads. It twists and turns through the foothills outside Tanner Springs, past fields and farms, with the mountains miles away in the background. I let my body work with the bike, leaning deep into the curves. I try as hard as I can to force Samantha's image out of my mind. But in doing so, my thoughts turn toward the past. Toward the most fucked-up period of my life. The time I try hardest to forget. And the one person I wish more than anything I'd never laid eyes on.

I speed up a little, taking the curves faster than I should. I'm trying to outrun my thoughts, I know. I don't like thinking about any of this. Remembering that my brother might still be here if I hadn't fucked up so badly. If I hadn't let my guard down and betrayed him.

I drive and drive, working hard to empty my mind of everything that's chasing after me. After a while, I feel the tension start to ease a little from between my shoulder blades. Eventually I slow to a near-stop on the wide open, deserted road, then turn the bike around and head back into town, feeling almost human again.

On my way back to the clubhouse, I pass through downtown and happen to drive by The Lion's Tap, one of the local dive bars. It's just past three in the afternoon, at the beginning of early happy hour for the drunks. The usual crowd of smokers is hanging around by the front entrance.

As I ride by, a familiar figure happens to catch my eye. Before I register who it is, a petite blonde happens to turn around at the sound of my bike. We lock eyes.

Anita.

She gives me the finger, her face contorting into an ugly scowl, then sneers and turns back toward her group.

All the anger and rage I rode out of town to escape comes flooding back.

As if the universe wants to hammer home the fact that I have no business messing with Samantha Jennings.

A few minutes later I slam into the clubhouse, pushing open the door so hard I think for a second I've broken it. At the bar, Jewel and Skid's old lady Rena jump.

"Jesus, Hawk," Jewel gasps, putting her hand to her chest. "You scared me half to death."

"Sorry," I scowl. "Give me a beer and a shot."

I catch Jewel raising her eyebrows slightly at Rena. "Sure thing," she murmurs, and heads off down the bar to grab my drinks.

"Hey, Hawk," Rena says cautiously. She's sitting a couple of stools down. She doesn't come into the club much, so she must be waiting for Skid.

"Hey." It comes out louder and harsher than I want it to, and I feel bad, but fuck it.

"Okaayyy," Rena drawls, and rolls her eyes. "I'm gonna just go over there for a while." Her stool scrapes on the floor as she gets up. I don't glance over.

Jewel sets my beer and my shot in front of me. I slam the shot and motion for another, which she gives me without a word. When I slam that, too, she gives me a questioning look.

"Just set the bottle up here," I say darkly. "It'll be quicker."

Behind me, I can hear Rena whispering softly with a couple of the club girls. Looks like I've successfully scared away the women. Good.

Unfortunately, the men won't be so easy. A couple minutes later, Thorn comes ambling up and sits down next to me. "Hey, brother, all right there?"

"Not in the mood for conversation," I mutter.

"Jaysus, who pissed in your corn flakes?" he chuckles, undeterred. Thorn loves weird American expressions, especially when he can use them to piss one of us off.

"Fuck off, Thorn," I bite out.

"Ah, come on. You got a drink in front of ya, you've got my fine company. What more can you want, then?" He raises his own beer and gives me a cheesy grin.

"I swear to God, Thorn, I will beat you to death if you try to cheer me up."

He whistles. "Some people are just determined to see the world as all bad. Come on, lad. Turn that frown…"

"Thorn, you mother—"

"Hey, brothers," Brick's deep voice interrupts, probably saving Thorn from a broken jaw. "Jewel," he calls. "Beer."

"Careful," Thorn warns him. "Hawk's in a foul mood."

Brick snorts. "What else is new?" He leans against the bar and takes the beer from Jewel. "So, have you heard?" he continues. "Rock, Angel, Ghost, and Geno met with Ozzy and his crew. Looks like they reached a deal with the Death Devils to take the guns off our hands."

"That's great," Thorn nods. "When are we doing the transfer?"

"Rock set up a meet at a spot right on the border between our two territories. They'll meet us there with a couple of their trucks," Brick replies. "Should be in a day or two."

Even though I'm in no mood to celebrate anything, this is good news. "I'll be glad to get that shit out of our hands," I admit.

"Yeah," Thorn agrees. "Things are getting too hot right now. I keep expecting the news that Holloway's goons have found out the warehouse is ours and raided it."

"That piece of shit dead fish-eyed little fuck," Brick glowers. "Every time I see his face I want to punch it."

"You and me both," I say, and allow myself just the slightest smile. Beating the shit out of Jarred Holloway is maybe the only thing that would put me in a good mood right now.

"There's our boy!" Thorn crows. "All sunshines and rainbows."

"Jesus Christ, Thorn, you are fucking annoying," I growl, but he's so goddamn ridiculous I find my mood lifting in spite of myself.

"Hey," another voice says behind us. I turn to see Angel. "Saddle up. Rock wants you guys to head out to the warehouse and take inventory of what we've got out there."

"Now?" Brick asked, his face registering confusion. "I thought the gun transfer wasn't for a couple days."

"Rock wants to get shit ready," Angel replies. "I think maybe he's getting antsy. Doesn't want the Devils to change their minds. Wants to nail down the details, get it done as soon as we can."

Good thing I'm only a couple of shots down, I think. I was working on getting good and hammered. Twenty minutes from now and I'd be in no shape to drive.

I stand up, as do Brick and Thorn. With a twinkle in his eye, Thorn grabs the whiskey bottle that was sitting in front of me. Then three of us head outside and drive out to the warehouse, to take stock of the guns.

Chapter 13

SAMANTHA

"Sam, these are just so, so gorgeous," Jenna gushes. "I really don't know how to thank you enough!"

We're sitting on the couch in the main room of the carriage house, my laptop hooked up to a large monitor on the coffee table. Jenna's here to pick out the final photos for the wedding album. She and Cas have already looked at the pictures online, but I like to do this part face to face. I want to make sure that clients feel free to tell me about any changes or adjustments they'd like to make.

"It was a really fun wedding to photograph," I tell her truthfully. "Not to mention one of the most interesting ones I've ever done."

Jenna's eyes sparkle. "Yeah, the Lords are definitely something else," she laughs. "I wasn't quite sure what to expect myself, to tell you the truth. Our wedding was the first time I've seen the men try to clean up and act respectable for a little while. Not sure they pulled it off."

I laugh, then watch as Jenna continues to click through the images herself. I take notes as she makes a comment on one photo or another.

Eventually, Jenna comes to the pictures of Hawk playing the guitar. I draw in a sharp breath as one after another, I see his strong hands stroking the strings — the same hands that made me gasp with pleasure. The sensual lips that burned my skin. The dancing, mocking eyes that turned dark and stormy as he pulled me against him…

When I came back to the carriage house from getting yelled at a second time by Gram, Hawk was gone. I don't know what I expected, exactly. I didn't actually ask him to stay until I got back. I *wanted* him to, but it felt too weird and needy to actually say it out loud. So instead I just said, "I have to go," and hoped for the best.

Frankly, when I got back and saw he was gone, part of me was a little bit relieved. Before Lourdes knocked, we were definitely about to… Well, let's just say that as turned on as I was, I wasn't going to stop him, whatever he did. My body had completely short-circuited my brain and all I could think about was having Hawk push himself deep inside me, deep enough to stop the ache that was driving me mad with longing. Having to stop and go talk to Gram had brought me at least part of the way back to my senses. But I'm pretty sure that if Hawk had still been there when I got back, we would definitely have finished what we started.

As relieved as part of me had been, I still spent the rest of that day horny and frustrated. And when night fell and I couldn't take it anymore, I fumbled in the drawer of my nightstand and found my battery-powered boyfriend. It wasn't enough — it wasn't *nearly* enough — but at least it allowed me to fall asleep that night without going crazy. Thinking about it now, heat begins to grow between my legs.

"These pictures of Hawk are amazing," Jenna says, cutting into my thoughts.

I swallow quickly and look at her with a bright, probably stupid-looking smile. "You think so?"

"Yes. I've never seen him quite like this. He's usually so…" Jenna frowns for a moment. "Brooding." She eyes me curiously. "Did you happen to talk to him at the wedding at all?"

Ha. "Um, yes, I did have a… conversation with him." My face starts to grow hot.

"Oh, well then, you know what I mean," she laughs.

I should change the subject. Like, right away. But Jenna actually *knows* Hawk. Somehow, I can't stop myself. I want to talk about him. Even if it's just something superficial.

"Actually," I continue slowly. "He just came over to the house and fixed my grandmother's leaky faucet in the main house."

"Whoa, really?" Jenna asks, clearly astonished.

"Yeah," I nod. "I went to the hardware store to try to figure out how to fix it myself, and ran into him. Unfortunately Gram has kind of burned all her bridges with the handymen in town. She's never satisfied with their work and then she threatens not to pay them."

Jenna snorts. "That sounds about par for the course with Mrs. Jennings." Jenna, I found out about half an hour ago, is the daughter of the former mayor. She grew up just across the street — in the house that is now occupied by the much-despised Cantwells. So Jenna's known Gram for years. I find myself wanting to ask her what happened to her father — why he left town and where he is. But I sense it's not something I should talk about unless she brings it up first. I don't want to upset her if it's something painful.

"So, Hawk volunteered to come over here and fix it for you?" Jenna whistles softly. "Wow. That's not something I would expect him to do. Hawk's kind of the 'keeps to himself' type. Though, he is amazing at fixing things."

My heart skips a beat when she says this. Somehow, the notion that he came and fixed Gram's sink for *me* — not just because he's the kind of guy who does stuff like this — makes me feel almost giddy. But then I remember how he left without even saying goodbye.

"Yeah. It was pretty nice of him." I try to sound casual, ignoring the lump forming in my stomach. "And you should have seen the fur fly when Gram came home and found a huge tattooed guy in a leather vest in her kitchen. I thought she was going to spontaneously combust."

Jenna starts to giggle. "Oh, my gosh. I would have paid money to see that!"

"I think the humor was lost on me at the time," I say wryly. "Since I was the one she ended up taking it out on. She still hasn't forgiven me, even though I reminded her that I got her sink fixed for free."

Jenna and I work on the wedding photos for a little longer, but at this point it's mostly chatting about our lives and getting to know each other better. She tells me about growing up in Tanner Springs, leaving as soon as she could manage it, and then eventually coming back and getting together with Cas, whom she'd had a fling with when she was barely out of high school.

"Oh, wow," I exclaim when she tells me that Noah was the result of that fling. "So you haven't been together since Noah was a baby?"

"No, not at all. In fact," Jenna says with a pained look, "I didn't even tell Cas I was pregnant at the time. When I came back to town, Noah was already four. I didn't tell Cas he was the father until a couple months later. By then we were back together. I was petrified that he would be so angry he'd break up with me." Her the pain in her face gives way to relief, mixed with love. "I never could have imagined that we'd end up like this — Cas and me together, with two children. Sometimes I still can't believe it all worked out."

"That's quite a happily ever after," I remark, wishing I believed in them for myself.

"What about you?" Jenna asks, leaning back against the cushions of the couch. "How did you end up deciding to come to Tanner Springs?"

I tell her how I'm here allegedly to take care of Gram. She laughs uproariously at the idea that Gram would need taking care of.

"I know, it's ridiculous, right?" I laugh along with her. "To be honest, though, I think Gram was just lonely. As irritating as she can be, I think she just likes having someone besides Lourdes to boss around. And I'm pretty much the last family she has left. Well, other than my dad, who's her son. But God knows where he is. Neither one of us has seen him in years."

"Wow," Jenna breathes. "That's rough."

For a moment, I'm silent. I really want to ask her about her own father, but she doesn't offer any information, and something stops me.

"Was it hard to leave your life in the city?" Jenna asks then.

I snort softly. "A lot less hard than you'd think. It helped that I'd just gotten out of a two-year relationship when I found out my ex-fiancé was cheating on me."

"Oh, my God. Your *fiancé*. I can't imagine." Her eyes widen in sympathy.

"Yeah. Even better, it was with our freaking wedding planner." I shrug and laugh. "Though she wasn't the first one, to be fair. Just the first one I found out about."

"Oh, Sam, I'm so sorry. You must have been *destroyed*." She shakes her head.

"Well, let's just say I needed a change of scenery after that. My ex is a fairly well-known sports writer. So I ran into people who knew him pretty often." I smirk at her. "So you see why leaving the city had its attractions."

"I think you and I both came here looking to escape," she tells me. "I hope your story ends up as well as mine has."

"I'm not sure that's possible," I grin. "Seems like you hit the jackpot."

"Oh!" she says suddenly. "That reminds me. I have a question to ask you. I just started a job a couple months ago working for the school district's community ed program. I was wondering — and if this is something you don't want to do, that's fine — would you be at all interested in teaching a community ed class in photography? It would only be one night a week," she continues hastily. "And it doesn't pay much, unfortunately. But they've had people asking for a class like that, and of course I immediately thought of you."

"Hmm…" I hum, thinking for a moment. "Actually, it sort of sounds like fun. Plus, maybe if it ends up going well and becomes more of a regular thing, Gram will get off my back about getting a 'real' job." I look at Jenna. "Sure. I'd be up for that."

"Excellent!" she beams happily. "And who knows, maybe you'll end up getting some more business from it!"

Chapter 14

HAWK

The MC gets to the warehouse the day of the meet-up to pick up the guns, to discover that the locks have been broken off the doors. Inside, it doesn't take long for us to confirm the worst: all the crates of 9mm pistols and AR-15s are gone.

"Jesus fucking Christ goddamn son of a bitch!" Angel shouts, running his hands through his hair. We're standing in the warehouse, looking around at the empty space where the crates were stacked the last time Brick, Thorn, and I were out here. Some of the other shit is gone, too, but it's clearly the guns they were after.

Rock is angrier than I've ever seen him. He turns to me. "When were you here last?" he barks.

"Two days ago," Brick says. "To pack everything up for transport. Everything was locked up tight when we left."

Tweak comes up to us, looking grim. "Looks like the surveillance cams have been shot out. The ones I've looked at so far, anyway."

"Goddamnit," Rock seethes. "Go check the rest of them. See if you can get any footage out of them at all. We need to figure out who did this."

"You think it's possible the Death Devils did this?" Ghost asks, his face a mask of anger. "You think they're fucking playing us?"

"It's possible. Hell, anything's possible." Rock is silent for a moment, but he looks like he's going to explode. "But if it was them, it's not like anything we've seen from them before."

"Yeah." I nod. "It's been pretty much peaceful coexistence with the Devils up until now. The Iron Spiders, on the other hand…" I don't bother to finish my sentence. The rest of the men know exactly what I'm thinking. The Spiders have been trying to push into our territory for a while now. They've got plenty of motive to try to fuck with us.

"How would they know where this warehouse is?" Gunner bites out.

"I dunno. Shit, maybe they have someone working for them in our territory." After all, they managed to turn Charlie Hurt, Jenna's old landlord. He's dead now, but the Spiders could have other people spying for us. It stands to reason that they'd try, anyway.

"Anyone else it could be?" Angel asks.

"No one else really has the capacity to do this kind of a job," Ghost growls. "It's got to be one of them."

"Well, we're to be at the drop in less than an hour," Thorn mutters. "I think we're gonna find out whether the Devils are playing us by what happens when we tell them we don't have their inventory."

Grimly, I realize we may be headed for a war. The stony faces of the other brothers tell me they're thinking the same thing.

The meet-up is just outside our territory, at an old factory that looks like it's been closed for many years. When we get there, we drive inside a huge open doorway that looks like it was made to accommodate large construction vehicles. Inside, a couple dozen Death Devils are there, with two vans to transport the guns we don't have.

All of the Lords, on the other hand, have come on bikes. There was no reason to bring trucks, having nothing to transport in them. And what trucks and vans offer in terms of protection, they lose by being slow. If there's gonna be trouble, I'd rather be on a bike than in a cage any day.

A large, deeply-tanned man with long dark hair and a thick beard stands in the middle of them, wearing a plaid shirt and a leather cut. I don't even need to look at closely to know his lapel patch says "president." I've never met Ozzy before, but he commands a respect among his men that's immediately evident by the way they stand and wait for him to speak. It's like he's the center of gravity or something.

If Ozzy and the Death Devils are behind the break-in and gun theft at our warehouse, then he's the best goddamn actor I've ever seen in my life. The exact moment when he realizes we haven't brought any vehicles large enough to transport product is obvious. He throws Rock a sharp and suspicious look of anger. The rest of the men come to stand in a disciplined half-circle around him. It's pretty clear they're getting ready for the possibility of violence.

Ozzy's face grows dark and steely when Rock tells him about the break-in. He is fucking *pissed*.

"We had a deal, Rock." His voice is cold, menacing. "You promised us guns. We promised our people guns. We now have a problem." It's not clear whether he believes us, or whether he thinks this is a set-up.

Rock takes a step forward. "Ozzy. Our clubs have never had a problem with each other. I don't plan to start one now." He looks briefly over at Angel. "We think we have a pretty good idea who did this. They will pay. We will get the guns back. And we will deliver them to you as soon as we do. The deal is still on. It's just been unfortunately delayed."

Ozzy seems to relax just slightly. The change in his face is hardly visible, but it's there. "Spiders?" he asks.

Rock nods once. "We think so."

Ozzy's eyes narrow, his lip curling slightly. He says nothing, but it's pretty clear what he thinks of them.

"As I said, we promised our people a shipment of guns," he says. "I am a man of my word. I don't appreciate being made to go back on it."

Then he shouldn't have made a promise until the guns were in his possession, I think.

Rock's voice grows hard. "Soon, Ozzy. We'll have the guns back very soon. I'll be in touch."

He nods once, not waiting for an answer from the other president. Then Rock turns and lifts his chin to us, the signal that it's time to go. We walk out in silence, in a show of confidence, but I'm half-expecting a shout, or gunshots, to ring out behind us. The fact that Ozzy lets us leave without any problem is a good sign. But even so, this is not a great way to begin a solid future partnership if necessary against the Spiders.

"Well," Brick murmurs to me as we walk toward the bikes, "I guess we know what happens next. The Spiders just bought themselves a war."

Chapter 15

SAMANTHA

Saturday morning — the six-month anniversary of my arrival in Tanner Springs — starts out bright, sunny, and gorgeous. It's a perfect day for what I've been told is one of the highlights of the year: the annual library fundraiser.

The fundraiser was started over fifteen years ago by the Tanner Springs Public Library's board of directors. I know this because my grandmother told me all about it at length two nights ago. She was on the board when the fundraiser was launched the first year, and naturally she credits herself with its continued success. Gram doesn't serve on the board anymore, and apparently hasn't even gone to the fundraiser for the past two years. But she still takes it very seriously, and contributes a hefty amount to the cause annually. As her granddaughter, it wasn't even a question in her mind that I would be going.

Truth be told, I'm sort of looking forward to it. This is exactly the sort of small-town event I've really never experienced before, having grown up in a city. On the morning of the fundraiser, about an hour after it's supposed to start, I put on my favorite sundress, pull on some comfortable yet pretty sandals, and set out for the walk downtown.

By the time I'm a little more than a block away, I can hear and see that the event is already in full swing. For the occasion, the main street has been blocked off with wooden barricades. As I get closer I see that four entire blocks have been taken over by tents and booths. Literally hundreds of people line the street — men, women, children of all ages. Music blares from somewhere over on the other end. There's so much to see I'm a little overwhelmed. Gram told me this was a big deal, but I had no idea it was *this* big.

As I get inside the barricade, I realize I need a plan in order to see everything. I'm going to start on one end and walk down one side of the street from beginning to end, and then loop back around and come back on the other side. I decided before I left that I wouldn't bring my camera, not wanting to have to lug around a heavy bag all day, but now

I'm regretting that decision. There will be so many opportunities for great shots here that I'm tempted to go back and grab it. *You can always run home later and come back with it,* I reason with myself. For once I'm going to try to just enjoy the occasion and be in the moment, instead of always being behind the camera trying to capture it for the future.

The tempting scent of popcorn fills the air, and even though I had breakfast already, my stomach rumbles in appreciation. I resist the urge to get a bag, and instead start strolling down the right hand side of the street, weaving my way through the throngs of people. It's a full-scale carnival without the rides. There are games, music, crafts, face painting, balloons… the whole works. I pass by a couple of high-school age kids doing an amazing juggling act with bowling pins, and a woman in a long, flowery dress playing guitar and singing folk music. A couple of older ladies are standing at a table selling pies and jars of homemade jams and jellies. Further on, there's a ring-toss game manned by a very bored-looking teenager, and a middle-aged woman selling really pretty handmade jewelry.

Eventually, I walk the entire four blocks and come to the end and the other barricade blocking the street. On this end, there's even a raised stage with large speakers sitting on the ground on either side of it. There's nothing happening on the stage right now, but it looks there will be some sort of band or other performance there later, judging from the microphone stands and chairs that are already set up on and around it.

I cross to the other side of the street and start back in the other direction. About halfway back, I see a large booth with a big, colorful awning over it. The name of the library is emblazoned on the awning, and a handful of people are staffing it, handing out brochures about the library and pointing out a large box for donations. To the left of the booth, there's a huge bookshelf full of all kinds of books. A sign on the shelf says the books are free to take, and suggests a donation in exchange.

I slow down and scan the people under the awning. This is my one actual task of the day: I've promised Gram that I would stop by the library's booth and talk to RuthEllen Hanson about a job. I've been putting it off as long as I can, but if I don't do it today I'll never hear the end of it from Gram. Sighing, I approach the booth and ask a twenty-something woman in trendy horn-rims if Ms. Hanson is here. She gestures at a neat-as-a-pin woman who looks to be in her mid-sixties, with a short, roundish hair style and pale blue eyes.

"Ms. Hanson?" I say when I'm just a couple of feet away. She turns and looks at me expectantly. "I'm Samantha Jennings. Phyllis Jennings's granddaughter?"

"Oh, yes," she nods, sticking out a slightly bird-like hand for me to shake. "Phyllis told me you'd be getting in touch with me." Ms. Hanson glances around for a second. "Why don't we go over there in front of the pharmacy and talk, away from all this noise?"

I follow her to the varnished wood and iron bench that sits in front of Krebs Pharmacy and sit down beside her. Ms. Hanson folds her hands in her lap and gives me a polite smile. "So, are you enjoying our little festival?" she asks, gesturing with her chin.

"Yes, actually, I am," I say truthfully. "It's charming. It's a lot bigger than I thought it would be."

"Well, we are very proud of this event," she answers, obviously pleased. "It's truly one of *the* events that the citizens of Tanner Springs look forward to every year. Of course," she continues with a wink, "Your grandmother is convinced that she is single-handedly responsible for its success."

I laugh. "That does sound like Gram. Honestly, I'm surprised she doesn't come to it anymore, to give everyone a chance to congratulate her."

"Yes, well." Ms. Hanson's eyes cloud over a little. "Your grandmother has retreated quite a bit from public life since Richard died. She took his death very hard, even though it wasn't unexpected. He had been sick for a while."

"Excuse me… Richard?" I'm confused. My grandfather's name was George, and he's been dead for many years.

"Yes. Richard was your grandmother's… boyfriend, I guess you'd call him." She wrinkles her nose. "Such an undignified word to use with adults, though, don't you think? Your grandmother and he were together for a few years before he died of a lung disease." A sweet half-smile flits across her lips. "He was the only one who could ever get your grandmother to change her mind about something once she'd made it up. She loved him very much."

I'm stunned. "I had no idea," I admit. How could I not know my grandmother had had a boyfriend? How had she never talked about him with me? I had always just assumed that my grandfather was the last man she'd ever been with. And the few times she talked about him to me made it fairly clear they didn't have much of a relationship.

I'm both happy and sad about this news. I'm happy because it means that Gram did find love, after my grandfather's death. But I'm sad because she's probably still grieving for Richard. And she doesn't feel like she can talk about him with me. I feel like a terrible granddaughter, all of a sudden. *Maybe she doesn't want to talk about him,* I think. But then again, maybe it would make her happy to tell someone about him. Maybe it would make her feel like he's not so far away, to talk about her memories, and what they had together.

My throat tightens a little, thinking about all this. I resolve to try to be a little kinder to Gram, and to spend a little more time with her. And maybe, if I can figure out a way to bring it up without upsetting her, I can get her to talk about the man who sounds like he was the love of her life.

"Now. I know why you've come to see me, Samantha, and of course I do want to do everything I can to help Phyllis's granddaughter," Ms. Hanson says then, changing the subject. "I would truly love to be able to hire you on at the library."

She frowns slightly. "But I'm afraid that I won't have very many hours for you to start. The truth is, the staff we already have can easily cover all the shifts, and I already have a couple of part-timers who want to go full-time as soon as it's possible."

I tip my head to the side in confusion. "You're not looking to hire anyone? But Gram said…"

"No, I'm afraid not," she says apologetically. "But as I said, I certainly do want to help you in any way I can…"

"Oh, but I'm not looking for a job," I assure her, my face breaking into a grin. "I've got my own photography business that I'm setting up, and it's actually going quite well." I breathe out a sigh of relief. "Gram just doesn't think photography is a real job, so she keeps trying to get me hired somewhere, even though I keep telling her I'm not interested."

RuthEllen bursts into laughter. "Of course she does! That's classic Phyllis." Relief floods her features. "Oh, I'm very happy to hear that. I wasn't sure what I was going to tell my part-timers about why I was hiring a new person instead of giving them more hours." She stops laughing then. "Oh, but what will we tell your grandmother?"

"Well," I begin, thinking for a moment, "I did actually just talk to someone who works at the community education office about teaching a photography course. I can tell Gram that I turned you down because the hours you were offering me clashed with the times the class was being offered."

Ms. Hanson seems delighted with this plan. "That's perfect," she says, clapping her hands. "Your grandmother can be a force of nature, you know. But I would hate to hurt her feelings."

The two of us get up from the bench and walk back toward the library booth. As we do, I happen to glance across the street, and see something I hadn't noticed before. A group of tattooed, leather-clad men are setting up a *massive* black box on wheels made of thick metal, with a large grate welded on top. I recognize it instantly, because it's the biggest grill I've ever seen.

And the first time I saw it was at Cas and Jenna's wedding.

"Is that… the *Lords of Carnage* club?" I ask Ms. Hanson, stupefied.

"Yes, that's them," she says mildly. "They do the grilling for the fundraiser. Have done for quite a few years."

I turn to her, expecting to see an expression of… I don't know what. But she gives me an amused smile.

"Say what you will about them," she continues, "But they do cook one hell of a good hamburger."

As I stare in amazement, one of the men who had been bending down to put blocks under the grill's wheels straightens. My stomach flips at the sight.

It's Hawk.

HAWK

And before I can run away and pretend I don't see him, his head turns and his eyes lock on me like he knew I was there all along.

Chapter 16

SAMANTHA

Hawk ambles over, closing the distance between us quickly with his long legs. I suppress the urge to flee, and try desperately to look nonchalant.

"Hello," he says simply. He nods at Ms. Hanson. "RuthEllen," he says.

"Hello, Hawk," she replies. "Do you know Samantha Jennings?" she asks.

"I do."

"Please thank the club for their generosity again this year, Hawk," Ms. Hanson nods, gesturing toward the grill. Turning to me, she continues. "I really ought to get back to the booth, dear. So nice to have met you. Do come into the library sometime. We have quite a good selection of books on photography."

"I will," I promise her. I watch as she walks away, and then reluctantly turn my eyes back to Hawk.

"You look good," he says gruffly, nodding at my dress.

"Thank you," I say, as heat flushes my cheeks. I suddenly feel very conspicuous and exposed. Hawk's eyes grow dark as they slide over my figure. It feels almost like he's touching me without even lifting a finger. I resist the urge to squirm. I've never been so instantly affected by a man just *looking* at me.

"So, ah, the club is grilling the meat for the festival?" I manage to say, sure that I sound like a complete idiot. "That's not exactly what I would have expected you guys to be doing on a Saturday afternoon."

He shrugs, but his eyes are still lingering on the curve of my breasts. "It's good PR. Keeps the town from wanting to run us out."

As I look at his face, I notice that his handsome features seem tense. Preoccupied. He's not as cocky and flirtatious with me as he usually is. He's less infuriating this way, but it's strangely… disappointing.

I find myself wanting to ask him what's wrong. But I don't. Because I don't think he'd tell me anyway.

When I saw him from across the street, the first thing I wanted to do was run. Or maybe throw something at him, and ask him why he just disappeared without a trace from the carriage house when I went to talk to Gram. I don't know what I expected from my next encounter with Hawk, but it wasn't *this*. He's so serious, so completely unlike I've ever seen him. It's much easier to know how to act around him when he's being a jerk, I realize. I want him to say something completely inappropriate, so I can hide behind my righteous anger. But I can tell that's not going to happen.

So, because I don't know how to act when he's not being a cocky ass, for some reason *I* start acting flirtatious.

"Who's doing the grilling?" I say in a teasing way that sounds forced and artificial, even to me. "I'm imagining one of you guys in an apron and a chef's hat."

But Hawk barely seems to hear me. "How's the leak in your grandma's kitchen?" he asks. The tone of his voice makes it clear he's just phoning this conversation in. My heart sinks a little bit. I know I'm not the most interesting person in the world, but it seems pretty clear I'm boring him. I have no idea why he bothered to come over and talk to me in the first place.

"Um, fine. Thanks again," I stammer, and hope I'm not turning beet red as my thoughts turn to what happened *after* he fixed the sink.

"That's good," Hawk says absently, running a hand through his dark blond hair.

Just then, one of the other men calls to him. "Hawk!" He turns his head.

"I need to go help them finish setting up," he explains.

"Okay," I say softly. Part of me is relieved that this disaster of a conversation is over. But a bigger part of me is battling a wave of disappointment that this is apparently how it ends.

"Okay then," he nods, his expression still tense and preoccupied. He turns to go, but after a beat, he looks back at me. "Don't leave without saying goodbye," he mutters.

I don't know what to say to that. Or how to ignore the little thrill of excitement that goes up my spine at his words.

"Okay," I say in a small voice, but he's already swiveled back around and started walking back toward the grill.

I shiver, and close my eyes for a long second. Being around Hawk is like being pulled in by a tractor beam. He's all the way across the street and swallowed up in the crowd of other club members before my head starts to clear.

"Sam!" a familiar voice cries off to my right. I turn to see Jenna waving at me from about twenty feet away. She's pushing a stroller, with Mariana sitting in it and Noah skipping along next to her.

"Hey!" I smile and wave back. When she gets close, I squat down to the stroller. "Hi, Mariana!" The little sweetheart gives me a tiny wave and a wide, goofy grin. "Hi, Noah," I say to her older brother.

"Hi," he says back. "You're the photographer lady, right?"

"That's right," I nod. "Good memory. Are you enjoying the festival?"

"Yeah." Noah looks up at his mom. "We're going to do face painting next!"

"That sounds awesome," I enthuse. I put my hands on my knees and push myself back up to standing. "It's good to see you," I say to Jenna. "How've you been?"

"Great, thanks!" she says, and then glances toward where the club has set up shop. "Were you just talking to Hawk?" she asks me curiously.

"Um, yeah," I admit. I feel sheepish that she saw us together. But Jenna knows he came to fix Gram's sink, so maybe she'll just chalk it up to politeness. "He seems a little… off," I say. "I mean, kind of different than normal. Not that I know him well enough to know what's normal for him," I continue hastily. "Just… I don't know. Tense."

Jenna nods. "Cas is acting strange, too. I don't know what it is." She casts a worried look toward the group of men. "Funny how they're doing the festival like there's nothing wrong. But I get the feeling something is *definitely* wrong."

"You mean with the MC?"

"Yeah." Jenna reaches down absently and draws Noah to her.

I have no idea what kind of stuff the MC does, but suddenly the thought jumps into my head that Hawk could be in some kind of danger. I feel a little sick at the thought. "How much does Cas tell you? About the MC?" I find myself asking.

Jenna blows out a breath. "He tells me what he thinks I need to know. Most of the time, the guys try to keep the MC's business away from the women." She frowns. "Cas rarely brings that stuff home with him, but this time he has. I just hope everything's okay. But of course, if I ask him, he'll just tell me everything's fine."

Now I'm starting to worry. Hawk would never tell me anything about what was happening with the club, though, so it's stupid for me to even let myself think about it. Whatever is going on, it's not something I'm likely to ever know anything about.

"Hey," Jenna says then. "Why don't I introduce you to some of the women? You'll recognize some of them from the wedding, I'm sure."

Before I can say anything, Jenna's turned the stroller in the direction of the MC, where for the first time I notice a group of women gathered off to the side of where the men are setting up the grill. They've commandeered some picnic tables and are setting up blankets, playpens, and lawn chairs, clearly in anticipation of a long afternoon. Jenna introduces me to a bunch of women I definitely recognize from the farm. There's Rock's wife Trudy, a forty-something woman with pale blond hair and lots of eye makeup. There's Rena, who is trying to corral two rowdy boys and says she's with a man named Skid. There's a raven-haired beauty named

Carmen who says she's the wife of Geno, whose farm was where Cas and Jenna got married. Then there's the bartender I remember from the wedding, whose name is Jewel, and a few other women who are hanging around and helping with set-up.

As I'm chatting with the women, I happen to glance over and see that Hawk's eyes are on me, his expression impossible to read. I draw in a quick breath and quickly glance away.

"Mom," little Noah pipes up eventually. "You said we were going to do face painting!"

"You're right, bug," Jenna says. "Let's go over and get in line. It looks like there are a few people waiting already." She looks at me. "You up for waiting with me for a few minutes? Or do you want to be on your way?"

"No, I can come with you." I follow her as she maneuvers the stroller over to the face painting booth. As we go, Noah spontaneously take my hand and starts telling me about how he wants to get a tiger on his face. I tell him this is an excellent choice. When we get to the booth, it looks like we're fifth in line, so we settle in and start chatting as Noah immediately sees a school friend and runs over to say hello.

"Stay where I can see you, Noah," Jenna calls, and turns to me. "So, can I ask you a rude personal question?"

I snort. "Well, when you put it that way…"

"Sorry," she grins. "I just meant, I know this is personal, so you don't have to answer if you don't want to." Jenna peers at me, cocking her head. "Is there something going on between you and Hawk?"

I'm totally taken off guard by the blunt question. My mind is racing as I try to think of something to reply, when the sound of loud laugher behind us makes me turn my head.

"Oh, great," mutters Jenna. "Of course, *he* would have to bring his kids to get their faces painted at the exact same time."

Two groups behind us is a tall, dark-haired man with brilliantly white teeth, wearing perfectly-pressed khakis and a starched blue shirt rolled carefully up to the elbows. Beside him is a flawlessly made-up blond who looks like she spends most of her time with a personal trainer or at a spa. Two little girls with wispy white-blond hair stand beside them in matching floral dresses.

"Who's that?" I ask.

"It's the mayor. Jarred Holloway." Her lip curls. "And his gross, snooty wife, Annelise. Their younger daughter is in Noah's class at school." The shadow of something more than disgust — almost like sadness — crosses her face, but then in an instant it's gone.

Mayor Holloway is chatting and glad-handing everyone in arm's reach. It's clear he's in full campaign mode. When he gets down the line to us, he holds out his hand to me, but then freezes a little bit when he sees who I'm standing next to.

"Jenna," he nods politely, and then moves on to the next people.

"He's a snake," Jenna whispers to me. At that moment, I remember again that Jenna's dad used to be the mayor. Out of loyalty — but also because Holloway and his wife look about as fake as can be — I decide I don't like him at all.

We stand in line and continue to whisper as Holloway leaves his wife and kids to stand in line and walks off to greet other people. Jenna tells me that he has been eager to establish himself during his first year in office, and to make sure he's not a one-term mayor. "Part of his plan has been to tell the people how badly things in Tanner Springs were going downhill before he took over," she says in disgust. "Unfortunately, he seems to have the MC in his sights as a way to prove to folks that he can get things done."

"What do you mean?" I ask.

"He's been putting pressure on the club," she says with a worried look. "Cas tells me he doesn't think Holloway will be satisfied until he's run the Lords out of town completely."

"Can he do that?" I ask, looking over at the cluster of men standing around the grill. I remember what Hawk said to me about the festival being good PR for them.

"I don't know," she answers. "In the short term, no. But he's starting to mount a propaganda campaign against the Lords, and in the longer term, it might work." She sighs.

"Some of the women have said they're starting to get hostile looks around town from some of the residents."

As we watch, something surprising happens: Mayor Holloway makes a detour through the crowd and crosses the street, stopping just in front of Rock Anthony. "Uh-oh," Jenna murmurs.

"What do you think he's doing?" I ask. Holloway holds out his hand with a jovial smile. Rock frowns and slowly extends his to shake it.

"Like I said, he's a snake," Jenna sneers. "Whatever his plan is, he knows everyone here is watching him. He's playing the nice guy. Here, where it's all public."

I see Jenna glance back toward Holloway's wife, and my gaze follows hers. Annelise Holloway is chatting with a cluster of women behind us, and laughing at something one of them has said like it's the funniest thing she's heard in her life. She flips her hair back artfully, and her eyes dart away from the women as though to quickly take stock of who's watching. Jenna doesn't look away, and when Annelise notices us, she gives Jenna a tiny smirk and a finger wave.

"Looks like he's not the only one who knows how to work a crowd," I say.

"Nauseating, isn't it?" Jenna agrees.

"What's nauseating?" a low voice rumbles.

Chapter 17

HAWK

Samantha starts a little at my voice. Next to her, Jenna doesn't seem to notice her jumpiness and gives me a smile.

"Hey, Hawk," she says easily, and then leans in, lowering her voice. "We're just talking about our esteemed mayor and his wife."

I nod. "Nauseating's a good start."

"Are you getting in line to get your face painted?" Samantha says saucily. For the first time all day, I'm tempted to smile.

"Not really my style," I tell her. "You?"

Just then, the little kid standing in line behind us points at me. "I want arm tattoos," he announces to his mom. "Like him."

The mother glances up at me, and for just a second, I see a look of fear. Then she replaces it with a mask of politeness. "We don't point, Micah. But maybe we can ask if you can get them to paint some tattoos on your arm as well." She turns around to talk to the woman behind her, pulling the kid just a little closer to her.

"We're up!" Jenna says then, nodding toward the face-painting station. "Come on, Noah, let's go."

As Jenna herds her kids forward, I take Samantha by the arm and pull her aside. "Hey," I say. "I was wondering if I could talk to you."

"We're talking right now," she says. Her cheeks flush slightly.

"Away from here." I nod over to where the club's bikes are parked. "I thought maybe I could take you out on the bike."

Samantha's look of surprise is unmistakable. I don't blame her. I'm pretty fucking surprised myself.

But I need to see her. I need to talk to her.

"I'm wearing a dress," she points out a little unsteadily.

I look down at her skirt, and at the way that it skims her hips and flows out just a little around the curve of her thighs. My dick jumps.

"I think you'd be able to ride a short distance." My voice is thick. "I could drive you back to your place so you can change."

She's silent for so long I'm sure she's trying to figure out whether to just say no or to tear me a new asshole.

But then, her lips part, and a breathy "okay" comes out.

And even though my mind is preoccupied with the looming war with the Spiders, at that moment I'm goddamn ecstatic.

"But I'm going to walk back to my place," she continues. "It's just a few blocks. I don't want to ride in this dress."

"Okay," I agree. I'll take whatever I can get. "I'll swing by in about thirty. Sound good?"

Wordlessly, she nods, and then turns to go tell Jenna she's leaving. I head back to the men and let them know I'm gonna take off for a couple hours. Out of the corner of my eye, I watch Jenna and Samantha as they talk. Jenna shoots me a look and raises her eyebrows. I don't react. Then Samantha turns and heads down the street toward her house. I watch her go and stare at her ass.

I have at least twenty-five minutes before I need to get on my bike, so I spend it hanging out with Brick and Gunner by the grill. They have a huge pile of hamburgers, brats, and hot dogs cooking by now, and people are starting to line up for plates. Brick is concentrating on flipping meat, and not talking much. Gunner, always comfortable in a crowd, chats with the housewives and the blue-hairs, disarming them with his ladykiller grin and making them forget the wall of tattoos that covers his skin from the neck down.

All around us, brothers and their families are talking, laughing, and eating. Today's a welcome distraction from what we know what's coming. The calm before the storm.

I guess that's why I want to see Samantha so bad today. Why it's been almost impossible to get her out of my mind. I don't want to think about tomorrow. I just want to think about today. Because tomorrow, we're walking into a war. A potential bloodbath, and none of us knows if we'll make it out safely.

And if something does happen to me, I want the memory of Samantha Jennings crying out my name in pleasure to flash through my brain at the end.

Wanting is dangerous.

I've been telling myself that — chanting it in my head like a fucking mantra — ever since the day I fixed Samantha's grandmother's sink for her. I've jacked off in the dark to thoughts of her more times than I can count. I know better than to do this. But when I saw her today, in that flowered sundress that manages to make her look innocent and sexy as fuck at the same time, any resolve I had to leave her alone flew out the goddamn window. I've never wanted anything as bad in my fucking life. It might be a mistake, but I don't give a fuck anymore.

Samantha Jennings is going to be mine. Just for a little while.

It's a testament to how full of Samantha my head is that I ignore maybe the biggest fucking warning the universe could have given me that this is bad idea.

As I'm leaving the fundraiser to go meet her at the carriage house, a familiar voice stops me on the way over to my bike.

"What's up, Hawk?" she drawls. I turn to see a petite blonde, her compact figure squeezed into a faded Harley Davidson tank top and a pair of worn, dirty-looking jean shorts that hug her scrawny ass. If anything, she looks even thinner than last time I saw her outside of the Lion's Tap. She's smoking a cigarette, her arms crossed in front of her.

"What do you want, Anita?" I growl. Of all the shit I am not in the mood for right now, *this* is at the top of my list.

She takes a couple of steps toward me. Up close, I can see that she's looking haggard, and her eyes are sleepy. I glance at the track marks on her arms, and my irritation mixes with frustration and a little bit of pity. She's using again. A lot, from the looks of it.

"Where's Connor?" I ask in spite of myself, but I'm pretty sure I know the answer. Anita doesn't like to be seen in public with a child. It makes her look less up to fuck.

She waves her cigarette dismissively. "He's with my brother," she says. "As if you care."

Shit. My hands clench into fists. If anything, Anita's brother is even more worthless than she is.

"I do care," I retort, but it's the wrong thing to say. As soon as the words are out of my mouth, something changes in her eyes. I recognize the expression. It's hope.

"That's not what I meant, Anita," I mutter.

Anita's face turns ugly then. She snorts in disgust. "Of course you don't give a shit. Typical. You want to look like a goddamn hero, but at the end of the day you're just like all the others."

"What do you want, Anita?" I repeat, biting out the words. There's no point in trying to have a conversation with her. I know that from bitter experience.

"You care so much about Connor, why don't you help me out?" she says defiantly. "He's not getting any younger. Growing all the time. Seems like he needs new shoes every week."

"Fine," I bark. She's probably just gonna spend the money on drugs or booze, but right now I'll do anything to shut her up and get her off my case. I reach into my pocket and peel off a few bills. She takes them from me with a snap of her wrist, not bothering to say a word of thanks.

"You're welcome," I say drily.

"Fuck you, Hawk," she spits out. "You think you're so superior." She turns to go, flipping me the bird and sauntering away like she thinks I'm looking at her ass.

I shake my head and lift a leg over my bike. Sitting down on the seat, I take a moment to massage some of the tension out of my neck. For probably the millionth time in my life, I wish I'd never laid eyes on Anita Reynolds.

Chapter 18

SAMANTHA

Hawk shows up at the carriage house about ten minutes later than he said he would be. I'm actually starting to wonder whether he just asked me to go on a ride with him as some sort of weird joke. I don't have his cell number, though, so I just have to sit and wait, and try not to feel like more of a fool with each passing minute.

When I do finally hear the sound of his bike outside, I'm relieved, but then I'm hit with a sudden wave of self-consciousness. Should I just go out and meet him? Should I wait for him to come to my door? I decide on the latter, because I'm hoping it will look like I haven't been staring out the window waiting for him. Which is exactly what I have been doing.

I race back into my bedroom and wait for his knock, just so I can nonchalantly stroll out to answer the door instead of immediately flinging it open. When I do open it, Hawk is looming in the doorway, his face a dark mask. He looks even more tense than he did when I left him at the festival. I open my mouth to ask him what's wrong, but before I can say a word, I'm slammed against him, his mouth crushing mine.

The kiss isn't soft, or gentle, but I don't want it to be. His lips are demanding, his relentless tongue forcing my mouth open and finding mine. A growl, deep in his throat, vibrates against my breasts as he crushes me to him, his hardness against my softness. It feels almost like the growl is coming from my own chest — like the boundaries of our bodies have collapsed. I moan into his mouth, the sound lost as he devours it. One hand reaches up and fists in my hair, and then for just a second pulls my face from his.

"This time, if someone knocks at the door, don't answer it," he rasps.

Then his mouth is back on mine. The softness of his lips and the roughness of his stubble are an electric combination. I want his mouth all over me, on every surface of my skin. In an instant, I'm burning up with desire. It's as though every second of wanting him since we first met has collapsed into this one moment.

When his lips leave mine to graze the soft skin of my neck, I'm panting and trying my best to stifle the cries that are threatening to rip from my throat. My vibrator had been doing overtime since I met Hawk, but Old Reliable is no substitute for the man himself — for being touched by these strong, rough hands that begin roaming over my body, setting my skin aflame. He cups my ass and pulls me against his hard length, and I let out a loud, unrestrained whimper of pleasure as my center finds what it wants. Then he's lifting me up, my legs wrapping around his waist. He carries me down the short hallway to my bedroom like he knows just where he's going, his lips still burning the skin of my face and neck.

Hawk's whole body is tense and hard with barely-contained lust, and my arms go to his muscled shoulders as I cling to him. His heart is slamming against his chest, his breathing fast and urgent in my ear. I feel impossibly tiny in his arms, completely under his control. And God, it feels so good. I don't want to think at all. I just want him to take me. I want nothing but his body and mine doing what they're desperate to do.

When he gets through the doorway to my bedroom, he stops just inside and pushes me against the wall. I'm still in his arms, my core pressed up against his hard, steely length, and it feels so good against my ache that I throw my head back and groan, my hips grinding against his. I could come just like this, and if he doesn't stop I will. I can't help it, my body wants what it wants. But instead he picks me up again and carries me to the bed, kneeling down on it with my legs still locked around him.

"Jesus, Samantha," he half-whispers, half-groans. "Jesus Christ, I've wanted to do this for so damn long."

His teeth nip at the skin of my neck, making me shiver. Then his hands move underneath the fabric of my camisole. The rough callouses on his fingers graze my skin as he slides it up, then finds the clasp of my bra and undoes it. I hold my breath as he finds the tender skin of my nipples with his thumbs and begins to tease them. I gasp and cling to him, pressing my forehead into his neck.

"Hawk," I whisper. "Oh, God…"

It's impossibly good. He rolls and pinches them, just hard enough that between my legs I start to throb almost painfully. I've never *needed* relief so badly before.

"I need to see you," he murmurs thickly. Without hesitating, I pull my shirt up over my head and remove my bra, tossing it on the floor. The look in his eyes when he pulls back to take me in is feral, almost frightening in its intensity. I resist the urge to cover myself, because even though I'm momentarily self-conscious, the lust in his eyes is so complete that it makes me feel like a goddess.

"Fuck," he hisses. "You're fucking gorgeous." His eyes lock on mine. "You know that, don't you?"

Heat floods my face. I can't open my mouth to respond.

"You're the most gorgeous fucking thing I've ever seen, Samantha." His head dips to my breasts, his lips closing over one nipple. I tense and arch my back toward his mouth, crying out again. My whole body is vibrating with need as his tongue swirls over the hardening bud. He moves to the other, lapping at the areolae, and if anything it's even more delicious. Between my legs, I can feel that I'm absolutely soaking my panties, and close to climaxing just from this as Hawk pushes me higher and higher.

Suddenly, I'm lying back on the bed and Hawk is pulling off my jeans. Breathlessly, I raise my hips to help him. Then in a flash, he's got his own shirt off and kicked his jeans to the side. The massive length of him springs free, pulsing and majestic. He quickly leans down, and I see the flash of a foil wrapper and hear the crinkle as he rips it open and slides a condom over himself.

As he kneels on the bed again, I arch my head back and open for him, unable to wait another second. Wordlessly, he moves between my legs and slides his head against my slick opening. I gasp loudly, and writhe toward him. Then his cock is spreading me open, filling me, stretching me, until Hawk is all the way inside me, his hands clamped tight around my hips.

I hear Hawk's fast, shallow breathing as he slides himself out, and then back inside me to the hilt. The velvety heat of his skin glides against my sensitive nub, sending waves of pleasure shooting through me with each thrust. My hands clutch at anything, grabbing the sheets frantically as he pushes me closer and closer to the edge. His groans reach me, seemingly far away, and I can actually *feel* him expand inside me as he continues to pump. We're moving together, breathing together, so close, so close…

"So good… Come for me, baby," he rasps, his voice low and insistent. "Come with me."

That's all it takes to push me over the edge. I scream his name and shatter, spasming around him as I come so hard it feels like I'm flying apart. Hawk thrusts once more, then twice, then empties himself deep inside me, roaring his release.

When I finally start to recompose myself and my breathing starts to slow, I risk a joke. "I thought you said a *bike* ride," I gasp.

Hawk laughs, low and sexy in his throat. "We can do that too, if you want," he chuckles. The last fifteen minutes or so seem to have helped him regain a little of his sense of humor.

"I'm not sure I could hold on without falling off," I tell him. My legs and arms are still quivering from the force of my orgasm. "Rain check?"

For a second, he stiffens, the movement so slight I wonder if I'm imagining it. "Sure," he says then. There's something off about his tone. Immediately I wonder if it's because this is just a hookup for him. I never should have said anything about there being a next time. Then I remember how tense he was looking earlier, and try to talk myself out of going down a rabbit hole I really don't want to fall into right now.

I just want to enjoy this moment. I don't want to spoil it. After all, it's not like I want anything else from him. I'm not exactly expecting him to pull out a ring and propose to me. As unbelievably earth-shattering as what just happened was, I'd be a fool to think it was anything more than just sex.

Which shouldn't make me feel quite as disappointed as I do.

Hawk pulls me to him for a deep, lingering kiss, and then releases me with a groan. "I could really use a glass of water." He swings his legs over the edge of the bed.

"I can get you some," I volunteer. "After all, it's my house."

"Nah, stay there. I'll find it. You want some?"

"Yes, please," I reply. Suddenly, I'm dying of thirst. I stretch my arms over my head with a big yawn. When he climbs out of the bed and walks out of the bedroom, all solid rippling muscles, I try not to let my jaw drop on the floor. I hear the sound of clinking glasses, then the faucet turning on and off a few times as he fills and drinks. Finally, he comes back in, a full glass in his hand. He stops at the doorway, naked and proud, and leans against the jamb, staring at me with a strange smirk on his face.

"What?" I ask defensively.

"That's a good look on you," he says, his eyes raking over my naked body.

I'm embarrassed, but I don't want him to know that. Instead, I try for bravado. "What, better than the sundress?" I joke. "Not sure this ensemble would be acceptable in polite company."

"Who said anything about *polite* company?" he growls, handing me the glass.

I take a few big gulps, and screw up my courage. "You're not so bad yourself," I dare to say.

Hawk grins at me and winks. "I know. I saw you staring at my magnificent ass." He nods over at the mirror above my dresser.

I don't have time to be mortified, because he lays down on the bed and takes the glass from me, setting it on the nightstand. "So," he murmurs, wiggling his eyebrows. "Ready for round two?"

If anything, it's better the second time than it was the first.

"Holy shit," I pant. "I think I've gotten enough cardio exercise for the entire year."

"You held up well," he says, the corners of his mouth turning up in this incredibly sexy way that makes my stomach flutter every time he does it. He sinks back against the pillows and I nestle into the crook of his arm. I like Hawk like this — all relaxed and kind of sweet, almost. It's a far cry from the cocky jackass I met at the wedding, or the sullen brooder I saw earlier today.

All the sex has made me feel boneless, and more relaxed than I've felt in I don't know how long.

And then I screw it up.

"So, I know you might not be able to tell me," I venture. "But is there something bothering you?" When Hawk doesn't immediately answer, I plunge in further. "I mean, you seemed kind of upset earlier. At the festival."

Hawk hasn't moved a hair. His breathing hasn't changed. But even so, somehow I can feel the temperature drop between us.

"No," he says. His tone is like a door slamming. "Nothing's wrong."

I change the subject, but the damage has been done. Gone is his bantering tone from earlier, and any attempt to engage him in conversation just confirms he's not really listening. About half an hour later, he detaches himself from me and says he needs to get going. I don't try to stop him — what would I say? Instead, I watch in silence as he pulls on his jeans, then his shirt, and slides on his boots.

"Hey," he says softly, just as he's getting ready to head out the door. "I'll be a little busy the next couple days. But I'll see you soon. Okay?" He leans down, and with a tenderness I would never have known he possessed, he kisses me, and strokes my jaw softly with his thumb.

I don't know why, but for some reason I feel like crying.

"Okay," I say. It comes out a little wobbly. "See you around."

Chapter 19

HAWK

My head's a fucking mess as I throttle up and turn the bike in the direction of my place.

Ever since the first time I sparred with Samantha at Ghost's wedding, I knew she wasn't someone I should let myself get involved with. Shit, for *so* many reasons. She just had this *thing* about her. It went beyond looks. She wasn't just hot — though I doubt she knows just how fucking sexy she is. She was sassy, driven, independent — she had me wanting to tease her and get her talking about herself almost as much as I wanted to fuck her.

I know it was stupid as shit not to just walk the other way. I should never have volunteered to fix her grandma's fucking sink, just to spend a little more time with her and maybe get her to let her guard down a little with me.

And then I went and did it anyway.

And now here I am.

And goddamn if fucking her just now wasn't about a thousand times better than I thought it would be.

In the weeks since I first saw Sam, I've told myself countless times that it was precisely because I wanted her so much that I couldn't have her. I don't think I've ever wanted anyone as much as her. Hell, I *know* I haven't. The more I tried to stay away from her, the more insistently she took up residence in my head. And every time I ran into her — which was inevitable in this goddamn town — just made it worse. Until I got to the point where I didn't care anymore. All I cared about was sinking myself inside her, and forgetting for a little while.

Just so happened that I picked the shittiest possible time to do it. Twenty-four hours from now, she could be hearing about my death, at the hands of a rival club. It wasn't fair to do that to her. Even though I'm not fool enough to think she's in love with me or anything like that, it would still scare her to death to come that close to the undercurrent of violence that's just an inevitable part of club life.

Selfish motherfucker. You selfish goddamn motherfucker.

I never should have let myself do this. I knew from the day I ran into her at the hardware store that she wanted me as much as I wanted her. I could see it in her eyes, in the way her breathing sped up when I got close to her. And I took advantage. I thought maybe she'd think I was less of a lowlife asshole if I did something nice for her.

But I wasn't doing it for her. I was doing it for myself.

Today when I saw her at the festival, I decided to hell with it. I decided to give us what I knew we both wanted. I was looking for a release. Because I was selfish. I should have just gone looking for one of the club girls. I could have closed my eyes with one of them and pretended it was Samantha under me when I came. But the fact is, I didn't.

Because I didn't want to leave this world without having Samantha Jennings in my arms one more time.

I've faced death before. You don't really get patched into an outlaw MC without accepting a certain amount of danger. And for the most part it doesn't bother me. Nobody knows when their number's gonna come up, but I'd sure as shit rather spend whatever time I have on this earth really living — even if it means my life's a little shorter as a result.

So I should have been able to resist her. I should never have been stupid enough to drag Sam into my world. Even for a little while. But the fact is, I wanted her too much for my own damn good. And especially for hers.

And now that I've had her? I want her even more.

My fucking traitor of a cock is stiffening in my jeans even now as I ride toward home, thinking about the softness of her thighs, and about how wet she was for me. We were both in too much of a hurry to take our time at it, and I'm already fantasizing about a next time, when I'll plunge my face between her legs and tease her with my tongue until she screams my name even louder than she did today.

No, I warn myself sternly. *You aren't doing that. You're going to stay away from her now.*

But I know I'm lying to myself. And my dick agrees.

Maybe Samantha will get lucky, I think to myself with a grim laugh. *Maybe I won't make it out alive tomorrow.*

And on that note, I pull up at my place, and head inside to go look for a bottle of whiskey.

Chapter 20

HAWK

The next day, my head is fucking pounding after spending most of my night in a bottle. I'm sober, and I'm awake, thanks to a gallon of strong coffee. But I feel like hell, and I'm in a foul-ass mood.

When I get to the clubhouse, most of the men are already there, tensely waiting for the signal to get moving. We're on our way to recover the guns the Iron Spiders stole from us — and to mete out some payback.

A few of the brothers had been doing some recon to try to find out where the Spiders had secreted away the crates. We already had some idea of where the Spiders' clubhouse was, down in a town called Circle Pines, a little more than an hour south of us. Ghost, Brick, and Beast had gone down there and done some sniffing around, and eventually discovered the Spiders' comings and goings to an old, abandoned meat packing plant on the north edge of town.

We take three vans, and close to twenty men, each vehicle driving different routes. I'm in the second one, with Brick, Tank, Thorn, and three other brothers. The drive down is tense and quiet, punctuated by shorts bursts of loud joking and laughter. Even with the recon done beforehand, we don't really know what we're getting into. Anything could be waiting for us, and we're prepared for the worst.

At about five minutes before the first van is due to arrive, Brick gets a text from Ghost. "We're good to go," Brick says, nodding tersely at Thorn to keep driving. "Rock's there. Be on the lookout," he tells us. "An ambush is always possible."

"Yeah," Thorn nods, and presses on the gas. The highway we're on doesn't have a lot of traffic, and at the moment we're alone on the road. A few minutes later, Brick gestures at an upcoming intersection and tells Thorn to turn right. We roll onto a potholed blacktop road, over a set of railroad tracks, and go another quarter mile before we see a cluster of buildings that must be our destination.

The plant itself consists of several mostly brick buildings of varying sizes, connected together. There's one large one with two tall smokestacks that looks like a generating station, and a bunch of others arranged around it, both small and large.

Brick points to one of the buildings off to the left. "There," he says. Just as he does, we see a rolling metal door open off to one side of it.

"Here we go," Tank mutters next to me. Thorn points the van toward the door and drives us through, nodding once as he recognizes our men on the inside letting us in. I exhale a little. So far, so good.

Thorn parks the van inside the door and we get out. The only light comes from some high clerestory windows up toward the ceiling, most of which are broken out. In spite of the small amount of fresh air coming through them, I'm immediately assaulted by a foul smell, faint but nauseating.

"Fucking stinks in here," Tank mutters next to me.

"That's the stench of Spider," jokes Thorn with a sneer.

Brick told us this was the building they saw Spiders going into and out of while doing recon. It's mostly a large, empty space, and looks and smells like it might have been where workers used to cut up animals when the plant was operating.

We walk over to where Rock and Angel are standing. Rock tells us the third van's here, and the men in it have already gotten into position as guards and lookouts. As far as Ghost and the men had been able to tell, the place isn't guarded by Spiders twenty-four-seven, but there's every possibility we might be watched or on security camera and have a limited time to get the guns out before the Spiders come for us.

"Okay, let's move," Rock says with urgency. We fan out and start searching. The building is huge, but it's mostly open space, so there aren't that many places to hide a shipment of guns, if they're here. I reflexively reach back for my Sig Sauer, to make sure it's securely tucked into my waistband, and move toward the back of the building where a series of corridors look like they might lead to something.

I don't find anything other than some old, dust-covered equipment and a bunch of broken glass. If the crates are in this building, they definitely aren't here. I'm starting to wonder if we've made a mistake somehow. Why the fuck would the Spiders store their shit in such a stupid, unsecured place?

"Here!" cries a voice from the other side of the building. I break into a jog and find a cluster of men standing in front of the rusted door of a walk-in refrigeration unit. There's a heavy steel lock on the handle.

Without ceremony, Rock raises his .357 Magnum and shoots the lock off from the side. Angel reaches over and flings open the door.

A blast of stench barrels toward us, and a couple of the men step back and swear in disgust.

But it turns out, we've hit the jackpot. The crates are there, all right. Eight cases of pistols, ARs, and ammunition.

But that's not all. There's boxes and boxes of shit, stacked up high against the walls. Tank reaches over and pulls off a loose lid on one of them, then peers inside.

"Drugs," he say. "Heroin, most likely."

"Fuck," Angel mutters. "It's gonna be hard to leave this shit. We could make bank taking it with us."

"Yeah," Brick nods with a gleam in his eye. "But we can make sure they don't make shit off it, anyway."

Now that we've found what we come for, we move quickly. Thorn pulls our van up next to the walk-in, and Beast pulls the second one in behind him. We divide the ammo and guns between each vehicle. When we're finished, Angel, Rock, and the others pile into theirs. "Go back by the alternate route," Rock orders us.

The first van drives toward the exit, and I look back into the refrigeration unit to see Thorn setting the anfo bomb Tweak sent with us. It's a mixture of ammonium nitrate and fuel oil. Tweak's rigged a remote detonator for the burner phone Thorn's carrying with him. The blast should be more than enough to destroy all the inventory in the refrigeration unit.

"Okay," he says urgently, getting to his feet. "Let's go." He climbs into the van's driver seat, and I throw closed the back doors. Thorn starts driving toward the exit, and the rest of us jog alongside the van to open the doors.

Just then Brick lets out a shout. "We got company!"

"Let's get moving!" I yell to the others. "Get in the truck!" The rolling door's still open, the van halfway outside, when the gunfire starts. It seems to be coming from all directions at once, and it's impossible to do anything but crouch low and try to get myself into the van before I try to start firing back.

Things go to shit fast. As far as I can tell, Spiders are firing at us from the brush, and our guys are firing at the Spiders. All I know is we have to get out now. My weapon's drawn, and I'm racing toward the truck when I hear Brick yell, "Watch out, Hawk!"

Before I have time to react there's a loud crack that somehow distinguishes itself from all the other sounds of gunfire — detaches itself in my mind like it's meant for me. Then I feel a strange tap on the right side of my back, like someone's hit me with a small rock. It makes no sense, and I instinctively start to reach back to figure out what it was, then realize how absurd that is and keep running. As I get closer to the van, a burning, aggravating sensation starts there, and starts to radiate outward.

Fuck. I'm shot.

I can hear the Spiders continue to shoot at us as Brick pulls me into the van and manages to slam the door behind me. I reach back now, and feel my back. It's wet.

"Shit, Hawk," Brick rasps. "That's gonna leave a mark."

"Fuck. Can Smiley take care of this?" I groan.

He shakes his head. "I don't think so, brother. This is gonna need surgery."

Goddamnit. That means the hospital. Which means I'm gonna have to make up some story about how this happened. Assuming we get there in time and I survive it, that is. I know without even asking we can't go anywhere else but Tanner Springs General. Any other hospital and we'd have the cops on our back asking questions.

Thorn jams the van into gear and whips it around so fast for second I think we're going to flip over on our side. The pain's starting to increase now, and through the fog of it I hear Tank ask me if I'm okay. I open my mouth to say yes when a fucking huge boom cuts me off, followed by another loud explosion. I turn with the others to see the smoke and shrapnel pouring out of the building from the anfo bomb Thorn just set off inside.

"Game on, motherfuckers," he grins back at us, holding up his phone.

I grin and try to give him a thumbs up, but a knife of pain slices through me. I groan and collapse sideways on the hard floor, gritting my teeth and settling in for the duration as Brick does what he can to stop the bleeding.

Chapter 21
SAMANTHA

I'm walking down the street at Mary Jane's maddeningly slow pace, waiting for her to do her business, when I get the call.

"Sam!" Jenna's breathless voice comes over the phone. "I'm so glad I got you right away!"

"What? What is it? Has something happened?"

Jenna sounds frantic, and I can't imagine what's wrong, but it's very clear *something* is.

"The club…" she begins, and then I hear her cover the phone and say something to someone on her end. When she comes back, I hear her take a deep breath and start again. "Something's happened with the club. I don't know all the details, but I do know they went on a run outside of their territory for some reason, and it went bad." She pauses, and continues in a softer voice. "Hawk got shot."

"Oh, my God!" I say, jerking so hard on the leash that Mary Jane lets out a yelp of surprise. "Jenna, where is he? Is he okay? What's happening?" I start to feel weak and sort of dizzy. My heart starts to speed up in my chest, so fast it's almost a tremor.

"He's at the hospital here in Tanner Springs. They brought him here — the club did — about half an hour ago, from what Cas says." Her voice is shaking, and it's clear she's doing her best to hold herself together. "I think they're taking him into surgery now. But that's all I know. We're not family, so they're not telling us much."

Hawk's hurt. The sentence is pounding in my brain like a throbbing headache. *Hawk's hurt.* I feel so shaky that for a moment I think I might lose my balance and fall to the ground, but I manage to keep my legs under me.

"Okay, I…" I choke out, and try to think of what the other words are. Normally imperious Mary Jane is eyeing me curiously. "I'll be there just as soon as I can," I finally manage to say. Tears spring to my eyes, and I have to fight to swallow the loud sob that's risen up in my throat. "Thanks for calling me, Jenna."

"I thought…" she pauses, her voice stricken. "Well, I just thought maybe you'd want to know. I'll be here waiting."

I take the phone away from my face with a trembling hand and turn back toward home, almost stumbling a couple of times. For once, Mary Jane is not resisting me and trying to get me to follow her lead. Instead, she trots beside me docilely, and I silently thank her.

Back inside the main house, I unleash the dog and bring her in to Gram, who's sitting at her dining room table with a stack of papers. When I tell her I'm going out and probably won't be back for dinner, she looks at me sharply, as though she can hear in my voice that there's something wrong. But if she does sense something's upsetting me, she doesn't say it, and I'm so relieved at not having to argue with her that I almost burst into tears right there.

By the time I've run across the lawn to the carriage house, I'm full-on ugly crying: wracking sobs that I am going to *have* to get under control if I have any hope of driving. I race inside and grip the kitchen counter hard to steady myself. I'm still sobbing uncontrollably, and I squeeze my eyes shut tight and try to concentrate on slowing my breathing. Eventually, I manage to get to the point where I don't think I'm going to hyperventilate. I go to the bathroom, splash cold water on my face until I start to feel a little calmer, and then go grab my keys and fly out the door to my car.

It's not until I'm almost halfway to the hospital that it occurs to me to question how Jenna knew to call me.

I haven't told her — or anyone — *anything* about Hawk and me. (*Not that there is a "Hawk and me." But even so…*) All Jenna knows is that he came to fix Gram's sink. Well, that and she saw Hawk and me talking together at the festival. But how she would put two and two together from only that is a mystery to me.

Right now, I can't think about any of that, though. Right now, I just need to know Hawk isn't dead. That he's going to be okay. That —.

A fresh round of sobs wells up in my throat, tears stinging my eyes. Angrily, I brush them away and swallow over and over, afraid I'll crash the car if I let myself start crying again. Five agonizing minutes later, I make it to the hospital, and almost run into the curb trying to park my car. I open the door and almost trip over my feet as I run toward the emergency entrance. Inside, I've stopped at the check-in desk and am breathlessly asking the older woman there how to get to Hawk when I hear Jenna's voice behind me.

I turn and fall into her arms in tears.

"It's okay," Jenna says in a soothing voice as she starts to rub my back. "He's in surgery now. We just have to wait. He'll be okay, Sam, he's strong as an ox. Nothing can take Hawk down."

She puts her arm around me walks me to where the rest of the club is waiting. Cas is there, and he gives me a brief nod and a one-finger wave. Noah and Mariana aren't there, and I'm guessing someone is babysitting them. I sit down next to Jenna in a row of chairs a few feet away from the men. I look down and notice that my hands are shaking.

"What happened?" I whisper.

"I'm not sure, exactly," Jenna murmurs. "I told you about all I know. The men left this morning on a run. When they got back, I got a call from Cas telling me something had gone wrong and that they had to bring Hawk here." She looks at me, worry creasing her brow even though she's trying to hide it. "They said he was shot in the back."

In the back... I imagine the bullet entering Hawk's spine, severing it. Hawk in a wheelchair. Hawk paralyzed. Hawk...

"Sam," Jenna says sharply, grabbing my hand. "Don't. Don't drive yourself crazy. You have to stay strong, okay? It does no good if you fall apart. Think good thoughts. Be strong." She shifts in her chair and looks at me intently. "You may not believe in praying, but there's no downside in putting positive thoughts, *hopeful* thoughts out into the universe."

Please let Hawk be okay, I pray, staring at the floor. *I don't care what happens between us. Just please let him be okay.* I close my eyes, and start to take deep breaths, repeating the mantra with every respiration. Inhale. *Please let Hawk be okay.* Exhale. *Please let Hawk be okay.* Inhale. *Please let Hawk be okay.* Exhale. *Please let Hawk be okay.*

I open my eyes, take another deep breath and let it out. For the first time, I look around and really notice my surroundings. The first thing I see is that a couple of the men, Cas included, are looking at me with unconcealed curiosity. Suddenly, I feel incredibly self-conscious. I have no place here. Not really. I'm not part of the club's family. I'm not really part of Hawk's life. Maybe it's ridiculous that I'm here. Maybe Hawk will wonder what I'm doing here when he gets out of surgery, and be pissed off that I'm acting like I'm his girlfriend or something.

"I — maybe I should go," I say awkwardly. I start to stand up, but Jenna catches my arm and pulls me back down.

"I think he'll want to see you, Sam," Jenna says softly. When I look over at her, she's staring at me with an expression I can't quite read.

"Look," she starts, "I don't know what's going on with the two of you… but clearly, there's *something* going on. Isn't there?"

I nod miserably.

"Well, then," she continues, her voice soothing, "Just stay here. And wait with the rest of us. And when Hawk's able to see people," — she carefully avoids saying *if*, I notice — "then go in and see him." She gives me a kind smile. "I bet he'll be pretty happy you're here."

Jenna suggests that we go get something to drink, and leads me toward the hospital cafeteria. I get a cup of absolutely terrible coffee and load it down with cream and sugar. We sit down at one of the tables, and I hold the warm styrofoam cup in my hand like it's precious, but for some reason I can't bring myself to drink it.

"I think whatever happened today is why Cas and Hawk and the others have seemed so tense lately," Jenna tells me.

She frowns in frustration. "Sometimes I really wish they'd tell us what the hell is going on, instead of trying to keep us safe all the time."

I think back to how preoccupied and gruff Hawk was the last time I saw him. And how, when he came to the carriage house, ostensibly to take me out for a ride, he pulled me inside and fucked me like it was our last day on earth.

It was only yesterday.

I shiver at the memory of his touch. I'd give anything to relive all of that again.

Maybe he did think it was his last day on earth, I realize suddenly.

I don't know how to feel about that.

"Can I ask you a question?" I ask Jenna after we've sat for a few moments in silence.

"Sure," she says. When I look up at her, it seems like she already knows what I'm going to ask.

"How did you know? To… call me?" It's all I can manage to say.

She laughs softly through her nose. "Well, I guess I didn't know for *sure*," she concedes. "But it seemed pretty obvious to me at the festival that there was *something* going on between the two of you." She shrugs. "I've honestly never seen Hawk act around any woman the way he acts around you."

"What do you mean?" I ask, genuinely confused. "All he did at the festival was grunt and brood, mostly."

"Oh, that's not true at all, Sam," Jenna laughs. "Besides. It's more just something in his eyes, I guess. And how he stands when he's close to you. It's like he's just totally aware of your presence, even if he's not talking to you directly. Besides," she continues, taking a sip of her black coffee and grimacing, "Hawk's not exactly the kind of guy to just volunteer to go fix some random person's sink for no reason. Especially not Phyllis Jennings."

"Huh." I guess it had never occurred to me that Hawk offered to fix Gram's sink out of anything other than — I don't know, *pity*, I guess. The thought that he might have done to spend time with *me* makes me feel giddy, and then I have to talk myself down because I don't want to get my hopes up if it's not true.

God, I am *so* messed up.

Jenna suggests we get back to the waiting room, so we stand up and take our disgusting coffees with us back down the long corridor toward the emergency entrance. When we get there, nothing has changed, and the men seem to have settled in for the long haul. I sit down in the chair I vacated a while ago and prepare to do the same. Jenna touches me softly on the shoulder and then goes over to talk to Cas.

I force myself not to look at the large clock on the wall, because seeing how slowly time is passing is threatening to drive me crazy. Instead, I sit and focus on a tuft of the beige hospital carpet in front of me that's been pulled loose. I stare at it like it's the only thing anchoring me to the earth. My breathing goes in, and out, and in and out. I start to feel cold, goosebumps rising on my arms. But I don't move. I can't move.

A doctor comes out, a slight, dark-complected man in green scrubs. He approaches the MC and Rock stands, then the others do as well. I practically bolt out of my seat and walk quickly toward them, standing just outside of the cluster of men.

"… fortunate that no vital organs were penetrated," he's saying. "The bullet passed through the muscles surrounding the abdomen, but did not enter the abdominal cavity. He's a very lucky man."

My legs grow weak under me, and for a second I feel faint with relief.

"How long until he's up and around doc?" Angel asks.

"Different people heal differently," the doctor replies. "That said, Mr. McCullough seems like a relatively healthy man, and he could be up and around within a matter of a couple of weeks."

"Can we see him?" Jenna breaks in.

"Mr. McCullough is still in recovery," he smiles. "Eventually they'll admit him to a room, and someone will come tell you where he is. When he is awake, we'll evaluate his condition, and it's possible that he could accept a visitor or two tonight. No guarantees, though, I'm afraid."

The doctor gives us a slight nod and disappears back through the emergency room doors. Jenna comes over to me and gives me a tight hug. "He's going to be okay, Sam," she murmurs.

I hug her back, and let out a shaky breath I didn't even know I'd been holding.

Then I go find a private bathroom, and burst into tears.

* * *

We wait a while longer. How long, I don't know. I pick up some magazines and flip blindly through them. I stare at my phone screen and try to play a game. I can't concentrate on anything.

Someone orders pizza. Jenna brings me a piece, but it tastes like greasy cardboard to me, so I throw it away.

Finally, right at the tail end of visiting hours, a short, round nurse with black ringlet curls comes out to see us. "You're here for Kaden McCullough?" she asks.

"Yeah," Rock says, getting to his feet.

"He's awake, and doing well. But visiting hours are almost over. I'll allow just two of you to see him. One at a time. And only for five minutes each."

Rock goes in first. He's gone for a little over ten minutes. I start to get antsy that because he's staying so long they won't let anyone else go in. But I have no reason to think I'll be the second person. I'm hanging on to a thread of hope, but I realize that it's not likely they'll choose me.

Finally Rock comes out. "He looks, good," he grunts. "He's gonna be fine."

A couple of people look around, but then Jenna stands.

"Sam is next," she says firmly, coming over to me and pulling me up by the arm.

I don't argue, and I don't wait for anyone to try to stop me.

Chapter 22

HAWK

Whatever the docs gave me for the pain, this shit is *good*.

I can't feel a damn thing. If I wasn't in this hospital bed, I'd question whether I'd even been shot. Everything that went down earlier today feels more like a dream than anything.

When I wake up, the first thing I can remember is one of the nurses — a short, stocky brunette with kind of a curly bowl cut — asking me if I had any family I'd like them to contact.

"No," I say, the drugs keeping my anger just far enough away not to reach me. "No family. Just my club."

She nods. "Well, there are quite a few people out in the waiting room who want to see you. But I'm not sure you're up for it just yet."

"I'm fine," I tell her. "It's all good."

She purses her lips. "Well. I'll see what I can do."

Then she's gone, and I close my eyes and drift off.

Then Rock's there.

"Hey, brother," he mutters. He pulls up a seat next to the bed. "We weren't sure you were gonna make it there for a while."

I try to laugh, but it makes me feel like something's coming loose, so I stop. "You're not gonna get rid of me that easily," I joke.

"Good deal."

"How's everyone else? What happened?"

"Everyone's good. We got everything out, managed to outrun them, no other injuries. 'Course," he continues, "This is only the beginning."

"Yeah." The Spiders aren't gonna let this go. Even though they deserved what they got. We all know this is the start of something bigger.

"You think we oughta go on lockdown?" I ask him.

"I do," he nods. "But we can't stay on lockdown forever. Still, I think as a precaution it's the best thing to do for now." He peers at me. "I'm gonna post a guard here, too. Just so we can cover all our bases until you get out of here. Doc says you might be in here for a week, maybe more."

"Bullshit," I scoff. "I'll be good to go in a day or two."

A rumble of laughter escapes him. "I don't doubt it, brother. You take care of yourself. They're gonna boot my ass out of here pretty soon, so I better get going."

I raise a weak finger at him. "Tell everyone to try to try to hold their shit together until I get back."

Rock snorts. "Will do, brother."

Then he's gone.

I close my eyes and drift off.

At some point, I think I hear the latch on the door again.

I open my eyes. It's the nurse.

"You have one more visitor tonight. But keep it short," she warns.

I look up, expecting Angel, or maybe Brick.

It's not Angel or Brick.

It's Samantha.

My chest tightens.

She moves into the room slowly, almost like she's nervous.

"Hey," I croak. "You're here."

"I —" she begins, and stops. "I mean, I heard —."

And then she bursts into tears.

Samantha sinks into the chair that Rock was sitting in a few minutes before.

"I'm sorry, I'm sorry. I'm just…" She takes a few deep, hitching breaths, then swallows painfully and gives me a bright, tremulous smile. "I'm just glad you're going to be okay," she quavers.

"I'll mend," I reply. I keep my voice gruff, because I'm afraid if I don't she'll hear how close it is to cracking. I'm so goddamn glad to see her right now I feel like I'm jumping out of my skin.

"Did… did you know you were going to maybe get hurt when you… um… came by yesterday?" she asks. Her cheeks flame, and in spite of all the drugs I'm on, my dick stirs at the memory.

"I didn't know I'd be hurt, obviously," I reply. "But yeah, I knew we were on our way to do something kind of dangerous."

"Why didn't you tell me?" she whispers. Before I can respond, she shakes her head almost violently. "No, no, I know. Jenna told me that Cas doesn't even tell *her*."

"It's not that I wanted to keep it from you, Sam," I say gently. "It's club business. It's something we vow to keep among us. Besides, you knowing would just make you less safe."

She nods quickly. "Okay. I get that. And it's not really my right to know, anyway. I have nothing to do with the club. I'm not like Jenna. I'm just…" she stops, and looks down at her hands.

Fuck. *She doesn't know,* I realize. She doesn't have any idea how I feel about her. That I've been fighting myself every damn step of the way on this.

"You're just the woman I wanted to spend time with right before I went into a situation I didn't know if I'd come out of alive," I say.

Sam's head snaps up to look at me. Her eyes are wide, and maybe a little hopeful.

I didn't mean to say any of that. I think the drugs are loosening my tongue.

"Sam, I'm sorry," I say, even though I don't really know what it is I'm sorry for. "I didn't mean to make you worry." In spite of myself, I crack a smile. "Though I can't say it hurts my feelings that you *were* worried."

She risks a small smile. "Well, I was," she admits. She glances toward the door. "I've been waiting out there for hours. With the rest of them. We were all worried sick."

"Come here," I say. She gets up and perches on the side of the bed.

"I need to talk to you about something," I say, realizing I don't have much time until they kick Samantha out. "I can't explain to you what happened, exactly. But the club is going into lockdown for a few days."

"Lockdown?" she says, wrinkling her nose. "What's that?"

"It means everyone goes to the clubhouse. Club members, old ladies, families. Everyone. No one comes in, no one leaves. It's a precautionary measure until we can be sure people aren't in any immediate danger." I hesitate. "I think you should go with them."

Her eyes widen. "Hawk, I can't. I have commitments. I'm starting to teach a community ed class. Besides," she continues, her eyes flicking away from mine. "No one really… I mean… No one really *connects* me to you, right? No one thinks we're… *together*, or anything."

"*I* think we're together," I say. Through the drug haze, part of me feels elated to say this, but part of me is scared shitless.

"You do?" she whispers.

"What about you?" I ask. I reach out my hand, which seems like a monumental effort. She takes it.

"I…" she begins. "I just thought…"

"Shhhh," I shush her. "What about you?"

She looks petrified for a second. Then her eyes meet mine, dark like they were when I took her in the carriage house.

Sam leans down and kisses me, a kiss that quickly turns deep and intense. My cock jumps beneath the thin sheets. Then she pulls away.

"I think so, too," she murmurs. She sits back and bites her lower lip. "But Hawk. I can't go into… lockdown." She stumbles over the word. "I really do think I'll be fine. No one, outside of you and, well, maybe the club now, knows about us. I really don't see how there can be any danger for me."

Reluctantly, I agree that she's probably safe. Even so, I decide I'll ask Rock to have one of the men keep an eye on her for a few days.

The nurse comes in then, looking impatient, and Sam squeezes my hand and follows her out. I lie there, my mind a fucked-up jumble of everything that's happened in the last thirty-six hours or so. Sam's beautiful face kissing me. Sam's body writhing under me as she comes. Brick hauling me into the van after I'm shot. Waking up in this hospital bed.

Suddenly, I'm fucking exhausted. I close my eyes, and start to drift into what will be a dreamless sleep. As I do, Sam's face floats there, a vision of hope.

Wanting is dangerous.

Chapter 23

HAWK

I end up having to stay in the hospital for five days. Sam comes to see me every single day without fail. Toward the end, I'm pretty antsy and anxious to get the hell out of there, even though I'm still not feeling all that great. Sam manages to calm me down and convince me to just let the doctors decide when I'm ready to leave. It doesn't hurt that she and I figure out a couple of creative ways to make use of the hospital bed — somehow not reopening my bullet wound in the process.

Meanwhile the club is in lockdown for four days. During that time, there's not a peep from the Spiders. Finally, Rock decides to lift the lockdown and give people the option of going home.

Two weeks pass, with the clubhouse on heightened surveillance, and still no response from them.

But we'd have to be fools to think it's not coming.

"Still no sign of retaliation from the Spiders," Rock is saying as he looks around the table. It's the first time we've had church since I got discharged from the hospital. "All the guns and ammo have been delivered to the Devils."

"So we're good with them?" I ask.

"Yeah. I think any damage is repaired now that they know we weren't trying to fuck with them and made good on the deal," Rock grunts. "Maybe, just maybe, there's an alliance to be had out of this. Oz is not happy with the Spiders."

So there might be a silver lining in this war with the Spiders. If we survive it, that is.

"We've still got brothers posted as guards outside the clubhouse twenty-four seven," Rock continues, gesturing toward the outside. "And Angel's sleeping here until further notice." Next to him, Angel nods, a steely look on his face.

"Funny Rock's got Angel staying here at the clubhouse, instead of himself," Brick mutters to me as we file out of church.

"Yeah." It is kind of fucked up. On the one hand, if something happened at the clubhouse in the middle of the night and Rock got killed, our club would be decapitated of its president in the middle of a war. On the other, if I was Rock, I wouldn't ask my VP to do anything I wasn't willing to do myself. I don't like it. But it ain't my place to say that. And hell, maybe Angel insisted on it being him. That decision's between the prez and his VP.

* * *

After church, I decide to head over to Rebel Ink, the local tattoo shop. It's where I've gotten all my art done for as long as I can remember. The owner, Chance, is a buddy of mine, and he's a goddamn genius with a needle. He only hires the best, which is why this shop has my loyalty.

I've been planning on getting this tat for a while now, and for some reason decided not to put it off any longer.

I park my bike in the small lot that belongs to the shop. There are five cars in the lot as well, two of which belong to people who work here. I'm glad to see the place doesn't look too busy. Rebel Ink occupies the bottom floor of a house, and above it is an apartment that Ghost's old lady Jenna rented before they got back together. The landlord and owner of the building, Charlie Hurt, used to live next door. That is, until a bunch of shady shit went down involving Jenna's dad, Hurt, and the Iron Spiders. Hurt ended up dead, and the ownership of this house and the one next door have been in limbo ever since.

I push open the front door and walk into the shop. The main room is smallish, with a raised front desk and an area off to the side. Low couches surround a coffee table stacked with ringed binders of designs. Two girls who look like they're barely out of high school are hunched over one of the binders, pointing at different pictures and chattering excitedly. They look up at me as I walk in and go silent, their eyes widening.

I ignore them and turn to Hannah Crescent, who's sitting at the front desk, her nose in her phone. She looks up and grins as she recognizes me.

"Hawk! Shit, haven't seen you around here in a while!" Hannah's fire-engine red hair is piled high on top of her head today in a kind of retro style. A tight navy-blue tank top leaves her arms bare, revealing the swirl of multicolored flower patterns covering the skin of her shoulders down to her forearms.

"Yeah. Been kind of busy," I tell her. "Had an unexpected vacation in the hospital."

"Wow. That's rough." She clucks her tongue but doesn't ask for more information. Hannah's discreet. She minds her own business. I like that about her.

"Chance or Sumner around?" I ask, leaning against the counter.

"Yeah, Chance is in back. Dez and Six are here, too, with customers. Sumner's coming in a little later. You here for some ink?"

I nod. "If he's got time for me."

"Ah, Chance always has time for the Lords," Hannah tells me. "I'll go back and grab him."

I watch her figure as she retreats down the hall. Hannah's got a great ass.

A few seconds later, she returns, with Chance following behind.

"Hawk," he drawls, and gives me a fist bump. "What can I do for you?"

"I've got an idea for a tattoo," I say, pulling out a worn piece of paper. "I'm thinking left forearm."

The design is something I drew a while ago. It's a black and white rendering of a guitar, with wings unfurling on either side of it. Down toward the bottom, in script, is a single word. A name.

Liam.

I've put this off for so long because thinking about my brother's death is something I've tried to avoid as much as possible over the years. But I don't want to avoid it any more. It's my fault he's gone. I shouldn't have the luxury of pretending it didn't happen. Liam's memory is something that should be with me all the time. And this is how I'm gonna make that happen.

"Nice drawing," Chance murmurs, whistling softly. "Yeah, I can do that. Come on back."

Chance leads me to his room, all the way at the back of the shop. I've spent more hours in here than I can count, over the years. His is the largest room, and sketches and photos of his work line the walls, including some of mine. I sit down in the chair and Chance adjusts the arm rest so my forearm is in a good position for him to work. The familiar smell of disinfectant wafts towards my nostrils.

Chance pushes his dark hair back from his face and takes another look at my drawing. "This will take a couple hours, but it's doable in one session for sure. What about colors?"

"Just black ink," I tell him, settling in. I wait as he sets himself up, adjusts the light, puts on his headband magnifier and pulls the tattoo gun next to him. Even though it's my forearm, Chance shaves the area to make sure there's no hair on the site. Then I sit back and let him work, the familiar prick of the needle almost soothing. For a while, there's no sound except the late seventies punk music playing over the speakers and the buzz of the tattoo machine.

Eventually, Chance sets the gun down. "I'm gonna take a little break," he says, stretching. "How've you been?"

"Not too bad." I tell him about my stint in the hospital, leaving out most of the details. Chance, like Hannah, is discreet, and knows better than to ask many questions about the MC's business. That's one of the reasons they've gotten so much of our business over the years.

"How about you?" I ask. "How's business been lately?"

"Good. Pretty busy." His brow furrows in annoyance. "As long as the goddamn building doesn't fall down around our heads, we're in good shape."

I laugh. "What do you mean?"

"Fuckin' Charlie Hurt's estate still isn't settled," he tells me, and rolls his eyes. "I guess the old asshole didn't have a lot of family, so it's been hard to figure out who inherits everything. Apparently the fucker had more money than anyone thought." He snorts. "You could have fooled me, as cheap as he was about upkeep on this place. Meanwhile, shit keeps breaking, things aren't up to code… And now with fuckin' Holloway as mayor, the city's on our asses worse than ever before." Chance shakes his head. "I'm tempted to just pack up the shop and move somewhere else, but I'm gonna stick around at least until they figure out who inherited this mess, so I can get reimbursed for all the money I've had to sink into repairs."

"Shit, I don't blame you," I say.

"Yeah. The next owner will be lucky if I don't punch him in the face," he says disgustedly. "Anyway, fuck it, enough of that," he continues, pulling his stool back toward me. "Let's get you finished up."

An hour later, the tattoo is done. He sits back and lets me look at the final product. I trust Chance, so instead of having him do a stencil of my drawing, I let him go freehand. The tattoo turns out even better than I expected. It feels right to have finally done it, though I know having it so visible means the bad memories will never be further away than a glance.

You deserve it, Liam. It's the least I can do.

I thank Chance, let him bandage me up, then go up front to pay and leave him a big tip.

Back outside, I hop on my bike and take out my phone to check the time. There's someone I want to go see, and I'm betting I know where she is.

Chapter 24
SAMANTHA

Tanner Springs Adult and Community Education
Introduction to Digital Photography

This class is geared toward the beginning photographer who wants to learn about their particular camera as well as photography concepts in general. Classes will devote time to hands on instruction with each student's camera as well as cover topics such as exposure, perspective, focus, and composition. Emphasis will be put on learning the skills needed to ensure you get the shot. Digital cameras can be intimidating – in this class you'll learn to master yours. Instructor: Samantha Jennings.

Five 2-hour sessions: Tuesdays, 6:00–8:00 p.m., Hawthorne Middle School.
Cost: $150. Class limit: 10.

Tonight is the second session of my photography class, so I already met all the students last week. There's Ronaldo, a charming and strikingly good-looking guy with black hair and dark eyes. There's Dennis, a slightly pudgy guy in his thirties with a receding hairline. Dennis already knows how to operate his digital camera, and seems to have signed up for this class only to challenge me whenever I explain a new concept to the class. There's Floyd and Gladys, an elderly couple who keep asking me questions about the best techniques for taking pictures of the naked body. There are a few middle-aged ladies who watch me with wide, determined eyes and follow everything I do like their lives depend on it. Finally, there's Annika, a twenty-something girl who during class last week mentioned that she's engaged no less than three times.

Tonight's class is about composition and focus. I start out by doing a short, hands-on explanation of the different focusing modes on the camera and talk for a while about how to use them to make interesting, engaging compositions. I take a few pictures of ordinary objects in the classroom, and demonstrate how changing the focus and composition of the shot can turn a simple photograph into a story. Then we go on a field trip outside, and I have them spend half an hour taking pictures around the middle school campus where the class is being held. Some focus on the plants that are landscaped around the school; others go over and take shots of the playground equipment. Dennis goes to the dumpsters by the back doors and starts taking artistic shots of garbage lying on the ground.

I wander from student to student, looking at the shots they've captured and making suggestions where I can. When the class is almost over, I herd them back into our room and recap some of the tips I've given them while we were outside.

"Okay, looks like our time's about up for tonight," I finally say, gesturing at the clock. "But before I let you go, let's go over the final project. This isn't a graded class, of course. But during the last session, you'll each be presenting a small portfolio of your work to your classmates, and giving a short five-minute presentation about a few of the photos and some of the technical choices you made when you took them, and why."

Dennis raises a bored hand. "Are you asking us to try to put words to our process?" he asks. "Isn't the point of photography that it's a *visual* medium, and that therefore it's a way of expressing what words cannot?"

I resist the urge to go over to Dennis and strangle him. "I'm not asking you to explain your artistic vision, Dennis," I reply patiently. "You'll simply be explaining in technical terms how you composed the shot. You don't need to explain why if you don't want to."

Gladys raises her hand. "Are we allowed to include nude shots in our portfolios?" she asks. A couple of the other students look slightly alarmed, their eyes darting first to her and then to me.

I don't even want to know, I think.

"Let's keep it G-rated," I suggest. "Any other questions?"

A few of the middle-aged ladies have things to ask. Finally, when no more hands are raised, I let them go. I'm gathering up my things when I realize that there's someone standing behind me. I turn to see Annika's petite form standing there, looking at me expectantly.

"Hi, Annika. Did you need something?"

"Um, yeah, I had a question." She's sort of bouncing up and down on the balls of her feet, whether from nervousness or excitement I can't tell. "So, I think maybe I mentioned last week that I'm engaged?" She holds up her left hand and shows me her engagement ring.

"Yes, I do think you mentioned that," I say. "Congratulations."

"Thank you!" Annika breaks into a wide, happy smile. "Well, so anyway, Justin and I — Justin's my fiancé — we were wanting to get some engagement photos done? But we don't really know any photographers. But then I realized, *you're* a photographer!" She beams at me, as if she's proud of herself for putting two and two together.

I can't help but laugh. She's sort of ditzy, but her enthusiasm is infectious. "Yes, I am," I smile.

"So, do you do engagement photos?" she asks. "I mean, I can tell you know what you're doing, and you're so nice! We don't want anything really fancy. There's this place out in the country? It's got this really cute old rustic barn and everything, and like, bales of hay? We thought it would be so neat to do it out there! Like, totally natural, not in a studio or anything."

"It sounds romantic," I agree, and pull out my card. "Here's my website," I tell her. "It's got all my information, including samples of my work and my rates. And I'll even give you a ten percent student discount if you decide you want to have me do your photos. If not, no hard feelings at all."

"Oh, thank you!" Annika says, clapping her hands. "I'll look at it with Justin. I'm so excited!"

"I can tell," I laugh. "I'll see you next week."

"Okay, bye!" She gives me another "I'm so excited" grin, and practically skips out of the room, waving the card at me one last time before she disappears. In spite of my instinctive dislike of all things engagements and weddings, I kind of hope she and Justin do decide to hire me to do their engagement photos. She's the giddiest bride-to-be I've ever met. I can hardly imagine what her fiancé will be like.

I haul my equipment bag through the school toward the parking lot, which will be deserted at this hour except for my hatchback. Only, when I get outside, I see it's not. Not quite, anyway.

There's one other vehicle in the lot. A familiar-looking motorcycle that's almost as big as my tiny car.

Next to it stands Hawk, a sexy smile curving one corner of his mouth.

"Want to cash in that rain check for a ride?" he asks.

Chapter 25

SAMANTHA

I've known Hawk for a while now, but this is the first time I've been on his motorcycle. Or any motorcycle, for that matter. I don't really have time to get nervous, though, because before I even say a word, he's slung one monstrous leg over the seat and is nodding at the empty spot behind him.

"Come on," he says. "Let's go."

I open the hatch of my car and stow my camera equipment, taking a quick look around to make sure no one's watching, but the lot's deserted except for us.

I climb on behind Hawk and put my feet on the pegs he points to. He starts up the bike and I jump a little at the sudden, loud roar. Instinctively, I wrap my arms around his waist to steady me as he puts the machine into gear. I feel the naked, raw power underneath me, between my legs. It's as though the bike is an extension of the man. Hard. Powerful. Dangerous.

We don't speak at all, we just ride. I watch as the town of Tanner Springs unfolds in front of us, close and immediate without the barrier of a car windshield. It's exhilarating. The cooling air chills my skin, and I snuggle tighter into Hawk's back and marvel at how I can feel the movement of his abs, even under his leather.

I have no idea how long we ride. He drives, and I lose myself in the sheer pleasure of the moment and of being with him. Eventually, he turns off onto a residential street, and pulls up at a house that I instinctively know must be his. A little thrill goes up my spine: he's never brought me here before. I tell myself not to read anything into it, but heat pools between my legs at the realization he probably hasn't brought me here to play Monopoly.

We're inside and his hands are lifting off my shirt and unhooking my bra before he even gets the door closed. Dimly, I notice a bandage on his left arm, but he's doing this thing with his teeth nipping at my earlobe, so any thought of asking him what it is flies out the window.

"Haven't seen you in two days," he growls against my ear. "Too fucking long." He rips his shirt off over his head with one hand, then thumbs open his jeans and drops them to the ground. His lips are on my breasts, teasing and biting at first one nipple and then the other, so ravenous it's almost painful. Hawk is like a man possessed, and I'm the possession. My body is for him, and I'm already soaking wet as I realize I'll do whatever he says.

Except first, there's something *I* want. My mouth is already watering at the thought.

Wordlessly, I slip out of his grasp and down onto my knees.

Looking up, I lock my eyes on Hawk's dark and stormy ones. He looks almost angry, but I know that's not what it is. He grabs a fistful of my hair as my hand closes over his huge pulsing shaft, my lips and tongue engulfing the velvety head. I moan softly, loving the way he feels in my mouth.

"Fuck," Hawk hisses.

I run my tongue along the sensitive ridge underneath, sucking softly as I take more of him in. There's no way I could ever take all of him in my mouth, but I compensate with my hand, giving him long strokes as I pull him in deeper, as deep as I can. His thighs are rigid, his hips thrusting just slightly as I stroke and suck him. For a few minutes he lets me do what I want, and I close my eyes, loving what I can do to him, wanting to bring him closer to the threshold, to the point of no return.

"Stop." The low command freezes me instantly. I look back up into his hooded eyes, so dark I can barely see the whites. He reaches down and pulls me up until I'm standing, and then my jeans are on the floor as well. "Take off your panties," he orders. I bite my lip and stare at him as I hook one thumb into the waistband, then tug just a little. I tease him, giving him just a glimpse of what's underneath, and his lips curl into a leer.

"You better get those off quick if you don't want to lose them," he growls. My nipples tauten as I realize he's about to rip them off me, and I hook my other thumb into them and pull them down, exposing myself to his lusting gaze.

"Bring yourself over here, Sam." It's not a request.

I take a step toward him. He grips me by the arms and suddenly I'm on the couch, lying prone with my legs spread. Hawk kneels and slides a teasing finger along my slick and aching lower lips. I moan loudly, my eyes half-closing at how good it feels. I'm already so close.

"Goddamn it, I love how wet you get for me," he snarls. Then he's between my legs, his tongue sliding between my lower lips.

"Hawk," I whisper. Already, I'm writhing uncontrollably at how good it feels. His tongue dips inside me, then emerges and begins to swirl patterns around my sensitive nub, just light enough to drive me crazy. I whimper and try desperately to move closer so he'll give me the relief I need. He holds me fast, though, so I can't move. I have to let him take his time, and just hope and pray he won't make me wait too long. The throb between my legs only increases as he teases and taunts me, so good and yet not enough, not nearly enough. I hear my low moans begin to grow higher, sharper, as I buck against his mouth and silently beg him for more. Then I realize I'm not begging silently at all. "Hawk, please," I moan, "please let me come."

He chuckles low in his throat, the vibrations teasing me as he continues to lick and lave. Finally, just as I think I'm going to lose my mind, he draws my tender bud softly between his lips and suckles me, sending a jolt of shockwaves through my entire body. I'm aware that I'm shouting but I can't do anything to stop it it, all I can do is just clutch at the cushions as I shudder and climax against his tongue.

I'm still shaking from the release when Hawk picks me up and pulls me onto his lap so I'm straddling him. He lowers me onto his hot shaft, filling me. I'm still contracting inside, and now my muscles pulse around him as he begins to thrust upward to meet me. We find our rhythm, Hawk kissing me deeply as he drives deep inside me, and it's so good, so good that everything else falls away and we ride the wave together, higher, higher, and suddenly he grabs my hips and slams himself into me hard, then empties himself inside me as we cry out together.

I'm quivering still as my mind starts to come out of the fog. My face is buried in his neck and Hawk is stroking my hair with one hand, his other arm clutched tight around me. Without a word, he gets to his feet and I wrap my legs around him. Hawk carries me to his bedroom and slips me under the covers with him. We lie there for a while, just kissing, Hawk still stroking my hair.

"How was your class?" he asks finally.

I burst out laughing.

"Very good, thank you," I say with mock formality.

"Glad to hear it," he smirks.

"So, what's this?" I ask, fingering the bandage on his forearm.

Hawk shrugs. "A new tattoo." He reaches over and pulls at the tape. "Actually, it's about time for me to take this off." He leans over and kisses me again. "I'll be right back."

I take advantage of his retreating form to stare at his gorgeous ass and muscled back. When he comes back a couple minutes later the bandage is off, revealing the art work beneath. It's a guitar like the one he was playing the day of the wedding, with a pair of wings behind it and a word written underneath.

Liam, I read silently.

I hesitate, wanting to ask him about the tattoo but knowing he might not want to talk about it. I remember the last time he mentioned having a brother. (*"Had,"* I correct myself.) I wonder if that's who Liam is. I know he's gone — though whether that means he's dead or just disappeared, I don't know. I swallow, nervous about doing the wrong thing and upsetting Hawk.

"It's beautiful," I say honestly.

"Liam was my brother." His voice is expressionless. Almost like he's reciting something from memory. I don't say anything, hoping he'll continue.

"He died ten years ago. When I was seventeen." Hawk nods at the tattoo. "The guitar I was playing at the wedding is his. *Was* his."

I wait for more.

Nothing comes.

"You must… miss him," I murmur softly, my heart breaking for him.

A beat.

"Yeah."

Hawk pulls me close to him, and I snuggle against his chest and listen as his breathing slows. This is the first time he's ever volunteered anything about his past. I swallow around the lump in my throat as I try to imagine how hard it must have been for him to lose his brother at such a young age. Being an only child, I don't really understand what it's like to have a sibling, much less to lose one. All I know is that Hawk wouldn't have gotten this tattoo if he didn't miss him.

Hawk is asleep now, his breath deep and even beside me. I turn and plant a soft kiss on his chest, then close my eyes.

Chapter 26

SAMANTHA

The next morning, a low, thick fog creeps into town. It hovers just outside Hawk's bedroom window like a weird, creepy spy.

The unsettling weather does nothing to kill Hawk's good mood, though. When I finally emerge out of my own fog of sleep, he's already awake, propped up on his elbow as he stares down at me.

"Finally," he grins. "I'm fucking starved. Let's go have breakfast."

It's a completely surreal experience riding a motorcycle through the fog. From my vantage point on the back of the bike, I can't see anything at all, so visually it seems like we're standing still. And yet my body can feel that we're moving through the thickened air. It's almost like what I'd imagine teleporting would feel like.

Seemingly by magic, we arrive in the nearly deserted parking lot of a neon-lit diner called Bucky's. I've never seen the place before, which adds to my sense of disorientation. Hawk waits for me to get off the bike, then takes my hand and leads me toward the building, which is actually an old train car. We walk past the long counter and slide into one of the only booths, toward the back. A waitress comes and brings us water and menus. I order coffee, orange juice, and French toast. Hawk orders a combo breakfast that ends up being so big it would last me for three meals.

I realize as we sit there that Hawk and I haven't really had a lot of casual chats since I met him. But somehow, the conversation flows completely naturally between us. He asks me about my life before coming to Tanner Springs, and I tell him about living in the city, my failed engagement, and wanting to make a clean break of things. I ask him about joining the Lords of Carnage, and he tells me about his early love of motorcycles, the modifications he's done on his own bike, and his dreams of someday opening up a custom bike shop.

"Wow," I marvel. "I had no idea."

"What?" he teases me. "Did you think I was nothing but a hot piece of ass?"

I laugh so hard I snort, causing the waitress to look over at me with an amused quirk of her brow. "No," I protest. "But I'm guessing there's a pretty big difference between someone who knows how to fix broken bikes, and someone who can actually design them. Sorry, but that's impressive." I take a sip of my coffee. It tastes good after the chill of being out in the fog. "Is that something you'd do with the club?"

"Maybe." He looks like he's contemplating it. "We're in the beginning stages of opening up a garage and repair shop. I haven't really talked to the men about expanding it to include customizations. But it's something that might work."

"You should," I urge him.

He frowns. "Maybe," he says again.

We sit in the booth talking long after we've both finished our breakfasts — so long that the fog lifts, and eventually the waitress stops coming by to refresh our coffee. By the time Hawk pays the bill and we get up to leave, a few people are starting to straggle in for lunch already.

"You want me to take you back to your car?" Hawk asks me when we're back at the bike. He wraps a strong arm around me and bends down to kiss me on the forehead.

"Yeah," I sigh. "I have some work to do today. Oh, but crap, I forgot that I left my purse at your place."

"No problem," he replies easily. "We'll swing by there first."

Now that the fog has lifted, it doesn't take me very long to start recognizing local landmarks and orient myself on the way back. I lean forward and tell Hawk how I was completely lost earlier, and he lets out an easy laugh that makes my heart jump to hear it. I've never seen Hawk this relaxed before. It makes me happy. Like maybe I have something to do with it.

As we turn back onto his street, I realize I'm smiling myself — a big, face-splitting grin that's probably due to a combination of delicious breakfast, a newly beautiful morning, and recent, mind-blowing sex.

If I ever believed in the dangers of tempting fate, it would be because of this moment.

"Shit," Hawk spits out, his whole body tensing. I frown and lean my head around to see what he's looking at.

Sitting in the driveway of his house is an old, rusted-out wreck of a car.

Sitting on the trunk of the car is a woman.

Sitting next to her is a small child.

The woman is thin to the point of being emaciated, and blond. Her clothes are too big for her, and look like they haven't been washed in a long time. When she sees me on the back of Hawk's bike, something happens to her face. Something ugly, and knowing. She slides down off the car, setting the little boy down on the ground a bit too roughly, and crosses her arms as she watches us pull in beside her car.

Hawk cuts the engine, his body still tense. "What do you want, Anita?" he asks her without preamble. His voice is cold with impatience and something like concealed fury.

She looks at him with disdain. "Well, I was coming here for a little help. Not that I expected anything from you." Her gaze flits to me. "New girlfriend?" she snorts.

"None of your goddamn business," Hawk mutters through clenched teeth.

"She's not bad looking, if you like her type," Anita comments drily. She turns to address me directly. "Honey, you're wasting your time with him. He's a pig. He can't be relied on. You want my advice, you should walk away now, before you get hurt."

"I make my own decisions, thanks," I reply curtly, but inside my blood is running cold. Is this an ex-girlfriend? Is Hawk the child's father? It certainly seems that way. But if so, how can he be so cold to them both?

Down on the ground, the little boy has found a small rock and starts to scrape at the dirt with it.

"I'm a little short on money until the end of the month," Anita says to Hawk with a smirk. "You wanna impress your new girlfriend and help me out for once? Connor's a growing boy. He needs to eat."

Hawk bursts into loud, laughter. "Right. I don't give my money to junkies."

Anita flinches. "You see?" she says, turning to me again. "He doesn't give a shit. He only cares about himself."

I'm starting to feel nauseated. This is a side of Hawk I've never seen before — an angry, callous side. My breathing speeds up, and suddenly, all I can think about is getting away from this. From *him*.

"I need to go get my purse," I say in a strangled voice, and rush to the front door, which thankfully Hawk has left unlocked. I run inside, grab my bag, and fly back outside and down the driveway.

"I'm gonna go," I mumble to no one in particular, feeling dazed and unsteady. I practically sprint past them both, ignoring Hawk's voice as he calls my name and tells me to come back. As soon as I'm out of earshot I burst into tears.

Everything I thought I knew about Hawk McCullough feels like a lie. Everything about the past weeks seems like an elaborate joke he's been playing on me to get me into bed. I can't believe how stupid I've been all this time, not to see something like this coming.

Hawk has a child. A little boy named Connor, whom he doesn't even care about enough to help support. A little boy he doesn't even care about enough to mention to me.

Chapter 27

HAWK

"Samantha!" I yell after her retreating form. "Fuck!" I look down at Connor and lower my voice. "Goddamnit, Anita," I seethe at her. "You need to stop this shit. Stop fucking with my life."

But Anita just flashes me a mouthful of graying teeth. "Should've just given me some money, Hawk. You woulda looked like a hero to your new fuck toy, and I woulda been on my way."

"Goddamnit," I swear softly to myself, and run a frustrated hand through my hair. "I'm not giving you more money, Anita. I know damn well you're not spending it on Connor."

She cocks her head and sneers. "You don't get to tell me what to do."

I can't help but laugh in disbelief. "With *my* money? Oh yes I fucking do."

Connor stands up now, and tugs at Anita's shorts. "Mama, I hungry," he says, right on cue. I'm not sure whether Anita put him up to this, or whether he's really hungry, but I'm not gonna let a little boy starve just because his mom's a piece of shit.

"Jesus Christ," I groan. "Wait here."

I go inside for a minute, and come back out with a peanut butter sandwich for the kid.

"What the hell is that?" Anita asks in disbelief.

I ignore her and kneel down in front of Connor. "You like peanut butter?" I ask him. He nods at me with wide eyes, and I hand him the sandwich. "Good. Here you go. It's crunchy. The best kind." Putting my hands on my knees, I stand up and face Anita. "I'm not giving you money. I'll call DeWitt's Grocery and have them put a hundred dollars on account for you. But this is the last time, Anita. Got me? The. Last. Time."

Anita snorts in disgust. "Fuck you, Hawk," she rasps.

"You're welcome. Now leave."

I don't wait to see if she does. I go inside and shut the door, locking it for good measure in case she tries to follow me. After a few minutes, I hear the sound of her shitty car driving away. Sighing with relief, I call DeWitt's and talk the manager into letting me buy a gift card for Anita that they'll keep at the service desk instead of giving it to her.

By the time I hang up, the good mood I was in earlier this morning has completely evaporated. I open the front door and take a seat outside on the front step. I blow out a breath and look at the fresh ink on my arm. Suddenly, I'm exhausted.

If I was a man who believed in signs, this would sure as hell be one of them.

Just when I'm starting to think this thing between me and Samantha could be more than just a good time, my past comes back to remind me that I don't deserve her.

Anita Reynolds was always a spitfire — a fiery, sexy, hot mess of a girl. Even in junior high, the old biddies of Tanner Springs were already talking about her. Whispering about how she was bound to turn out bad one day. With her flashing blue eyes and her bottle-blond hair, even at only five foot two, she stood out in a crowd. Anita practically *demanded* to be noticed.

Anita was the second girl I ever slept with. She was a year ahead of me in school, and a year behind my brother Liam. Anita had been eyeing me in the corridors of our high school, making sure to wear clothes skimpy and tight enough that any sixteen year-old boy with raging hormones could hardly fail to notice. She would wander by my locker between classes, or just happen to be sitting a table over from my group at lunch. She'd been attracting the notice of the male population long enough to know exactly when one was taking an interest in her — and exactly what to do to lure him in.

Hell yes, I wanted Anita. Shit, any straight adolescent boy with a pulse would give their left nut to fuck a hot piece of ass like her. So I wasn't exactly gonna waste a lot of time resisting when she made it clear she wanted me back.

I had just gotten my driver's license when we first hooked up. My first car was a shitty old Honda that barely ran and looked like hell. But a couple of days after I started driving it to school, Anita came up to me one day in between classes and asked me if I could drive her home that day.

Turned out, when we got to Anita's house, the rest of her family was conveniently absent. She led me down to her basement bedroom, where I took her, the smell of sex mixing with the faint must of the old carpet. The next day, I took her home again, and the day after that.

Anita was the first girl I ever knew who was always up for sex whenever I wanted it. She would do pretty much anything in bed, which was a definite plus for a horny young kid who was dying to live out all his adolescent sexual fantasies. We fucked like rabbits for a solid month, and thank God I wasn't stupid enough to ever risk it without a condom.

After a while, though, she started to get possessive and clingy, hanging out at my locker after class and demanding to know where I was whenever we weren't together. She started picking fights with me to get me to react, to see how far she could push me. Even though I was still attracted to her, I saw the writing on the wall and decided I needed to end things with her — even though my dick definitely disagreed with me.

Anita didn't take my brush-off lightly. She tried every trick in the book to get me back: waiting outside my car after school, calling me in tears late at night, sending me naked pics to remind me what I was giving up. When none of it worked, she started flirting with my friends to try to make me jealous. Finally, after a couple of months, she seemed to give up.

Then one day, I saw her talking to my brother Liam after school.

Liam was two years older than me, and at eighteen he was a senior in high school and just about ready to graduate. He was a little taller than me, and thinner, with the same dark blond hair and hazel eyes. Liam was also quieter and more intellectual than I was. He was really into music, and taught himself guitar at a young age. I don't know what he would have ended up doing if he'd lived, but I'm convinced he could have made a pretty good go at being a professional musician, if he'd wanted to.

Liam was more shy with women than I was, by a long shot. I'll never know for sure, but I suspect Anita might have been his first. At any rate, he fell head over heels for her, in the way a shy guy who's never had sex before might for the first girl who lets him into her pants. Pretty soon, the two of them were joined at the hip and spending all their time together.

Summer came, and Liam graduated from high school. Our drunk-ass mother didn't waste any time kicking him out of the double-wide the three of us lived in now that he was officially an adult. I didn't relish the prospect of dealing with her shit all by myself for two more years, so I decided to go with him. The two of us got an apartment together above a pizza place downtown. I got a job delivering for the pizza place, and Liam started working at a window manufacturing plant the next town over.

As the months passed, Anita and Liam's relationship started to turn sour. Liam had it bad for Anita. And Anita knew it. She tortured him the way a girl who knows how whipped her boyfriend is can do, just to prove to herself she had the power in the relationship. She'd pick fights with him that left him running in circles trying to figure out what he'd done wrong. She'd demand ridiculous displays of his love for her, and then shrug with indifference when he came through.

Pretty soon, Liam started to fear she was slipping away from him. He told me he worried that she might be cheating on him. By now, Anita was more or less living at our place — a fact I didn't like, but didn't know how to change. She'd walk around the apartment in the skimpiest clothes she could find to wear, especially when Liam was out somewhere. I knew she was doing it on purpose, trying to tempt me and drive me crazy. Though I always resisted the temptation, I'm ashamed to say her actions had their effect. Anita's body was smoking hot, and the memory of what it felt like to fuck her was recent enough that I guiltily pleasured myself in the shower to thoughts of her more than I care to admit.

I never, ever would have touched her, though. She was Liam's girl, and even if I didn't like it, their relationship was none of my business.

Then, one day Anita announced she was pregnant.

Liam, the poor fool, was over the goddamn moon when he found out. I guess maybe he thought Anita wouldn't leave him now that he was the father of her future child. Unfortunately, in the weeks after she told him the news, she became even more short-tempered and impatient around him than she had been before. She'd demand that he wait on her hand and foot, then complain that he was suffocating her.

My brother was in love, and bewildered, and was at a loss to figure out why he couldn't manage to do anything right and make her happy. He would confide in me about it all on the rare cases that it was just the two of us at home, and I would listen, try to be sympathetic, and pretend I wasn't well acquainted with her particular brand of bullshit. I was worried about him, though. A hundred times, I wanted to tell him to dump her, but now that she was pregnant I knew it was too late for that. Liam was a good, responsible guy. He never would have abandoned the mother of his child, no matter how bad things got between them.

Anita and I had never formally been a couple, and Liam never knew that we had hooked up. It felt like lying not to tell him she and I had a past, but I didn't know how to say anything without upsetting him. So instead, I just pretended none of it had ever happened. I found myself wondering whether it was partly my fault he was in this mess. Maybe if I'd told him right away that I suspected Anita was trying to hook up with him to make me jealous, I reasoned regretfully, he would have broken it off with her early on and wouldn't be saddled with a woman who clearly made him miserable.

School had started back up for me by then, and Liam had started working nights, and picking up extra shifts at the window factory to save up for the baby. One Friday night, Anita and Liam had a horrible screaming match of a fight, just as he was getting ready to go to work. Anita ended up storming out, and refused to answer Liam's repeated attempts to get her on her cell. Finally, he had to leave for his shift, looking more defeated and alone than I'd ever seen him. Right before he left, he made me promise to call him as soon as Anita came back, so he'd know she was safe.

Since I was the only one of my group of friends not living with his parents, our apartment had become a frequent hangout to party on the weekends. When Anita returned hours later, it was to a full-fledged blowout. At least three dozen people were crammed into our small place. The music was blaring and the drinks and recreational drugs were flowing. I wasn't happy to see her, but I was too drunk to care much. Not to mention, by then I had completely forgotten my promise to my brother that I'd call him when she came back.

Instead of disappearing into Liam's room as I expected her to do, Anita went into the kitchen and came out a few seconds later with a plastic cup full of dark liquid.

"You sure you should be drinking that?" I shouted above the music.

"Back off, Kaden," she yelled back testily. "It's only Coke."

I had my doubts, but I didn't care enough to pursue it. Instead, I concentrated on drinking and having a good time, and after a while, I forgot about Anita completely.

By the time things started to wind down, I was seriously fucked up and tired as shit. I told my friends to stay and party as long as they wanted, then stumbled to my bedroom to sleep it off. I peeled off my clothes and threw myself into bed, and was instantly down for the count.

I don't know how long I was out. But eventually I woke up in the dark to someone with long hair smelling like perfume getting in bed with me. I wasn't one to resist an opportunity for sex when I could get it, and pretty much all the girls at the party were hot. So when whoever it was kissed me, I started kissing back. I wasn't so drunk that I couldn't get it up, and when she reached down and started stroking my cock I wasn't about to stop her. Her mouth left mine, and then I felt her hot tongue lick a trail down my chest and past my stomach. When her lips wrapped around my cock, I groaned and fisted my hand in her hair. She began to suck, and I thrust my hips as slowly as I could, wanting to make it last.

"Anita?" The front door slammed out in the living room.

"Shit!" The girl going down on me pulled off and scrambled to sit up.

What the fuck?

I opened my eyes in horror to see Anita in the bed beside me.

A couple of light taps sounded on the door as it swung open. "Hey, Kaden, you awake?" Liam asked, his voice soft and apologetic.

The look on my brother's face when he finally registered the scene before him is something I'll never forget.

Thinking about it now, I stare down at the guitar tattoo on my forearm.

"I'm sorry, Liam," I whisper.

Chapter 28

SAMANTHA

I spend most of the day crying.

At first I think maybe I can focus on get some work done. Do something productive to distract myself. But I just can't stop thinking about this morning. I can't get the image of that angry, gaunt woman out of my head, and her little boy. Connor.

Hawk's son.

No matter how I try to come up with another explanation — some way to tell myself I'm overreacting — I just can't escape the fact that I misread what happened earlier today at Hawks house. But the evidence was right in front of me. I have to face it.

It's not that I'm jealous of an ex-girlfriend, although I have to admit I sort of am.

It's that he could be so completely unfeeling and uncaring about his own child.

I just can't ignore that. I can't ignore that it says something about who he is as a person. I'll never be able to trust him now, no matter what happens. I'll never be able to believe he wouldn't do something similar to me, if I somehow happened to get pregnant.

I have to stop seeing Hawk.

I don't know how I'll stand it, but I do.

The pain that hits me in the chest as I tell myself this is almost physical. I thought being cheated on by my fiancé was the worst possible way I would ever be hurt by a man. But somehow, this is so much more devastating. Even though it's not a betrayal of me, exactly.

It hurts, I realize, because Hawk hasn't even betrayed me yet. But now I'll always be afraid that eventually he will. And that makes me feel like all the oxygen is being sucked out of my lungs.

The phone rings a couple of times, but I don't answer it. I have an appointment later in the day — with a potential client for some family reunion photos — but I call and cancel it in between crying jags. After a while, I stop crying and fall into an exhausted sleep on the couch. Thankfully, I don't dream.

When I wake up, it's almost dark already. I've slept almost the entire day away. I feel a little better, and make myself some toast for dinner. Then I sit down and force myself to go through some emails and plan my day tomorrow.

I'm just about to shut my laptop and make myself go to bed when there's a soft knock at the door.

I tiptoe up to it and see Hawk's profile in shadow on the other side.

"I know you're in there, Samantha. Your car is here," he says.

"Go away."

"No."

"I'm not opening the door."

"If you don't open the door tonight, I'll just sleep here," he says. "Your grandma might take offense at me camping out in her back yard after a while."

I shut my eyes tight and will him to go away, but when I open them again it's clear he means what he says. I fling open the door.

"Go away," I say again.

"I need to talk to you."

"No."

"Please." His deep voice is gentle. Almost like a caress. I almost burst into tears again.

"I don't want to talk to you," I whisper.

"Sam."

He doesn't move, doesn't try to come in, but he makes it clear through his body language that he's not leaving, either. "That wasn't what you probably think it was," he says.

Somehow I manage to laugh. "Oh, no?" I ask bitterly and shake my head. "I have to admit, I can't think of a lot of alternative explanations to why a woman with a little boy would be coming to you asking for money. So you must have spent some time to come up with a really good one."

"Samantha." He doesn't get angry, or defensive. If anything, he just sounds tired. "Please. Just please let me in and give me five minutes. If you still don't believe me after what I have to say, then I guess I'll just have to live with that."

I open my mouth to say no again. I swear I do. So I have no idea why that's not what comes out.

I sigh.

"You promise to leave the next time I ask you to." It's not a question. It's the only way I'm letting him in this house.

He nods. "I promise, Sam. Just hear what I came here to say."

"When Liam found Anita in my bed, he assumed we'd been going behind his back for a while," Hawk is saying now, staring at his hands. "He was so upset he wouldn't listen to anything I tried to tell him." He shakes his head. "And Anita wasn't saying anything at all. Fuck, it didn't even seem like she cared all that much that we'd been caught. Maybe she thought I'd take her back if she and Liam broke up. I don't know.

"Liam went running out of the apartment. By the time I got some clothes on and ran after him, he'd sped away in his car." Hawk's voice goes ragged. "The next morning, the police came knocking. Liam had been in a one-car crash outside of town. He was going too fast around a corner and hit a tree. They said he probably died on impact." He looks down. "I'll never know whether he did it on purpose or not."

"Oh, my God," I breathe. I want to reach out, to touch him, but I'm afraid to move. I feel sick to my stomach at Hawk's words. It's clear to me he's not lying, at least about this part. He looks too destroyed. Like it just happened yesterday, instead of ten years ago.

"Not long after Liam died, Anita miscarried. At least, that's what she said." He rubs his jaw absently and finally looks at me, his eyes full of pain. "She wasn't far along enough to be showing. Looking back on it now, I'm not sure she ever really was pregnant. Or if she was, whether it was even Liam's kid."

"I'm so sorry, Hawk," I murmur. And it's true. My heart is breaking for him. Even though it happened so long ago, it's clear he's still living with the guilt.

Hawk leans back against the couch cushions. "Anita tried to start something back up with me after Liam died, if you can believe that shit." He blows out a disgusted breath, his face contorting into a snarl. "I told her to stay the fuck away from me and changed the locks on the apartment. After that, I didn't see her for a while. I heard she left town, then she was back, and somewhere along the line she got into drugs. I think she managed to piss off pretty much everyone she knew who wasn't a fucking deadbeat. Then she got pregnant." His jaw tenses. "Somehow managed to give birth to a healthy baby."

Connor.

"So… the little boy. He isn't yours?" I ask.

He sighs. "No. I don't know who Connor's dad is. Hell, I wouldn't be surprised if Anita doesn't, either."

I feel sick, and horrible for judging Hawk for something he didn't do.

"I feel damn sorry for that kid," Hawk says huskily. "Because as far as I can tell, Anita doesn't give two shits about him. And it could have been Liam's kid, you know? Maybe if my brother was still alive, it would have been his. Hell, Liam would have been fucking miserable with Anita, but at least he would have been a good dad to his son."

"So, that's why you give her money for food sometimes," I say softly.

"Yeah, I guess so." His expression is impossibly sad. "Probably doesn't do much good, but I just keep hoping it'll get Connor through for a little longer, and that maybe one day Anita will pull her shit together and start being a decent mother." He lets out a humorless laugh. "Not much chance of that, though."

I reach out and gingerly run a finger over the outline of Hawk's newest tattoo.

"Liam," I whisper, reading the word inscribed underneath the guitar. "Thank you for telling me, Hawk."

"I've never talked to anyone about it before." Hawk glances over at me.

"I'm honored," I say. "Truly."

His eyes meet mine. "I'm pretty sure my five minutes were up a while ago. Do you still want me to leave?"

In response, I move closer to him.

"No," I murmur, as he takes me in his arms. "I don't want you to leave."

Chapter 29

HAWK

A couple weeks later, I'm doing something I never would have imagined in a million years.

Samantha and I are on a fucking double date. With Ghost and Jenna.

Jenna suggested the whole thing, and Sam seemed so excited about the idea that after a while I started to come around to it, too. It seemed to make her happy to do something so normal with me. Like regular couples do. And hell, making Sam happy is worth anything, just to see the smile on her face.

The four of us ride out to a popular lakeside bar a few towns over, called The Lakeshore Tap. It's a place where bikers from all around the area like to meet after a long day on the road. Tonight, the place is hopping when we arrive, as it often is on the weekends. There's a stage inside where a band's going to be playing later. The four of us ask for a table outside on the patio, where we can enjoy our drinks and food with a view of the lake.

I haven't been on anything even resembling a date since I was in high school. And even then, I was only doing it to get into some chick's pants. At first, I feel conspicuous as fuck as we sit here, like I'm trying to fit into some weird "couple" mold. But little by little, I start to relax and enjoy myself. After all, it's a nice evening out, I've got a sexy as hell woman with me who keeps giving me these dazzling smiles, and I'm with one of my club brothers. Life is good.

Life is good.

I haven't had that thought in a very long time.

"I've never seen this many bikers at once," marvels Sam as she looks around. "Who are all these guys?"

"They're from clubs all over. Some of them are weekend warriors. Those guys over there are from the Death Devils," I say as I nod toward a large, loud group on the other side of the patio. "Some, I don't really recognize."

"Is it dangerous here?" Sam asks, wide-eyed. She doesn't know much about our club business, but I know she's thinking about how I got shot a while ago.

"Nah, it's okay," Ghost shrugs, leaning back in his chair. "This place is kind of neutral territory. The owner used to be the prez of one of the clubs the next state over, just across the border. He doesn't take any shit from anybody, and he doesn't hesitate to throw people out on their ass if they step over the line."

Inside, a four-piece band takes the stage to a smattering of applause. They start their first song, a cover of an old seventies classic rock song.

"Maybe you should try to get a gig here sometime," Sam says to me in a teasing tone.

"Not a chance," I tell her. "I only play guitar for myself, and for family on special occasions."

Across the table from us, Jenna smiles. "It's the world's loss, Hawk." She glances lovingly over at Ghost. "We were awfully lucky you agreed to play for our wedding. I'll never forget it."

"Okay then," I say gruffly, getting up. "Enough sap. Ghost, come out front and have a smoke with me."

Jenna and Sam laugh as the two of us push our chairs back, leaving them to whatever it is women talk about when their men aren't around.

Out in front, we go over to the bikes and lean against them. I offer Ghost a cigarette from my pack, which he takes.

"So, yeah," he says. "You and Sam, then."

"You gonna ride my ass?" I ask in a mock-angry voice.

Ghost laughs. "Of course not, brother. I'm happy for you. And for Jenna. She fucking *loves* Sam. I think she's excited as hell to have a close girlfriend around the club."

I don't say anything. Truth be told, I'm happier than I can ever remember being in my life, but I'm not ready to have a conversation about it.

Maybe sensing my reluctance, Ghost changes the subject. "Anyway, so I was talking to Angel earlier today. Sounds like we're gonna be looking at moving forward with the garage plans. Rock wants to talk about it at church in a couple of days."

"Good deal. It's about time we started moving forward on that." I take a pull on the smoke and blow it out. "You know, Sam had an idea a while back when I mentioned it to her. I was telling her how I've always wanted to design custom bikes. She said maybe we should expand the garage idea. Open a custom bike design workshop in the space, too."

Ghost thinks about it for a second and starts to nod. "That's not a bad idea. Shit, it's not like we don't have enough room at the warehouse. And I've seen what you've done to your bike and some of the other guys'."

"Yeah, and that's without a dedicated shop," I tell him. "I could do a lot more if I had the space and equipment to do it."

"Well, there'd sure as shit be demand for it," he agrees. "I can't think of another place around here that does any decent work of that kind. No way I'd ever trust any of them with my bike." He leans forward and claps me on the shoulder. "I think it's a great idea. It'd be a way to grow the garage and make a name for ourselves in the area. I bet the rest of the brothers would feel the same."

Shit, I'm starting to get excited about this. Without even meaning to, I start to dream about where things could be for me by this time next year. With Sam by my side, a new custom bike shop to get up and running... All of a sudden, it feels like my life's got a plan, a purpose, instead of me just living in the moment and trying not to think to much about the future or the past.

I finish my smoke and give Ghost a grin. "Come on, let's get back inside," I say. "I'm in the mood for another beer."

Later that night, the four of us ride home in the moonlight. Sam's arms are wrapped around me as she snuggles against my back for warmth. The moon is full, and so bright that I almost don't even need my headlamp.

Once we're back in Tanner Springs, Ghost gives me a wave and turns right toward his and Jenna's house. I continue straight toward my street. It's not even a question that Sam's staying the night with me, so I don't ask. I just drive up to my place, pull the bike into the garage, and take her hand to lead her inside. The two beers she had at the restaurant have made her sleepy, so we make slow, deliberate love until she cries out in the darkness and I crash over the edge with her.

Lying in bed afterwards, she softly traces the Lords of Carnage tattoo on my left pec. "Do all the club members have a tattoo like this?" she asks softly.

"Pretty much," I nod. "It's not a requirement, strictly speaking. But by the time you've gone through enough to get patched into the club, it's something you want to do."

"It's a lifelong commitment, then." She doesn't sound bothered, only curious.

"Yeah. Like a family. Maybe more so." I think about my own blood family, and what Sam's told me of hers. "Sometimes the family you choose ends up being more of a bond than the family you're born with, I guess."

I start to drift off to sleep, listening to the music of Sam's soft breathing beside me. As I do, I think about the two of us, and what the future might hold. Maybe someday, when we think of family, it will mean the two of us.

The loud crack of gunfire startles me awake, repeating so fast it can only be from a semi-auto rifle. I bolt upright, my brain struggling to understand what's happening. Then almost before I even know what I'm doing I'm pulling Sam to me and diving for the floor.

"Keep down!" I shout at her as the sound of shattering glass bursts in my ears like an explosion. Sam lets out a shriek and clings to me as I throw my body over hers to protect her.

Afterwards, I'll realize the whole thing probably only lasted five seconds or so before the squeal of tires and a revving engine signaled the gunmen's departure.

"Hawk!" Sam cries, her voice cracking with fright.

"It's okay, baby," I soothe. "It's okay. We're all right."

But the bastards who just tried to kill us won't be for long.

Chapter 30

SAMANTHA

The next day, I still start to shake uncontrollably whenever I think about the shootout at Hawk's place, and how close we came to being killed. When the rest of the club finds out what happened, Jenna immediately comes to the clubhouse to sit with me while the men have a meeting about it.

It's the first time I've been in the clubhouse. Any other time, I might have been intimidated or scared to come here, but under the circumstances it makes me feel safe and protected to have the entire club here, all around me. I remember back to when Hawk got shot, and how the club decided to go into lockdown. As I wait with Jenna while the men have what they call church, I ask her if she thinks they might do that again.

"I don't know," she says. "It's possible. It will depend on whether they think a lockdown is the best way to protect us all."

"Why would this happen?" I ask miserably. "Who would have done something like this?"

Jenna purses her lips. "Cas said this morning that he thinks someone from the Lakeshore Tap might have seen us last night and followed us back to Tanner Springs. When we split up, they could have just made a decision to follow you instead of us."

"Oh, my God!" I shudder, feeling suddenly cold. If they'd followed Jenna and Cas instead, the gunfire could have killed one of their kids, or one of them.

Jenna puts an arm around me. "It's okay. We're all safe now."

"Does the club have any idea who would have done this?"

Jenna nods grimly. "Yeah. I think they do. Cas also said he thinks this was just a warning. A kind of 'we know where you live' thing to spook the Lords. He said that if their aim had been to kill one of us, they probably would have just done that, instead of shooting up the front of one of our houses."

The door to the room they call the chapel opens, and the men come filing out. Hawk and Ghost come straight to us. Hawk sits down on the couch next to me.

"We're not going into lockdown," he tells me. "But you and I are going to stay here at the clubhouse for a few days." He strokes my cheek with his thumb. "My place is gonna need some repairs, and I don't want you going back to your grandma's right now."

I nod. I don't want her to be dragged into this — whatever it is.

"Hawk, can you please tell me what's going on?" I ask in a small voice.

"Just some problems with a rival club," he murmurs. "It'll get handled. But until then, I'm not letting you out of my sight."

"But… I can't just live here twenty-four seven indefinitely," I complain. "I'll lose clients. I've got the night class to teach. And photo shoots planned."

At first, Hawk argues with me and threatens to put his foot down. Eventually, I manage to convince him by promising I'll check in with him faithfully whenever I do anything or go anywhere, so he'll always know where I am.

A frown darkens his face as he considers this. Finally, he nods once, even though I can tell he doesn't want to.

"We're putting a GPS tracker on your phone, too, and connecting it to mine," he says, and it's not a question. "You keep that phone on your person at all times. No exceptions."

"I promise," I say immediately.

Even though I didn't want to be confined to the clubhouse twenty-four hours a day, I end up spending most of the morning here anyway. Truth be told, I'm a little nervous to go outside by myself. But eventually, I'm going to have to face the fact that I have things to do. Today is the day I'm supposed to meet Annika and her fiancé Justin for their engagement photo shoot. I need to go home and grab my equipment and pack some things for staying here the next few days.

Jenna stays with me until it's time to for me to go. I ask her if she'd mind driving me to the carriage house so I can go pick up my car. She drops me off in front of Gram's house, after giving me a hug and telling me to call her if I need anything. I decide to go through the main house instead of around the walkway to the back. I want to see Gram, just to make absolutely sure she's okay — even though I know there's probably nothing to worry about.

I find my grandmother upstairs in her bedroom suite, sitting on her favorite love seat and reading a novel, with Mary Jane at her feet. Her silver tea set is in front of her on the low coffee table, a half-drunk cup languishing on a saucer.

"Come sit with me for a bit, Samantha," she says when I appear in the doorway. "I haven't seen much of you lately."

It's true. Despite my promise to myself that I'd try to spend more time with her, I've been so busy — and let's face it, preoccupied with Hawk — that I haven't really done a very good job of being a better granddaughter. I cross the room and sit in the comfortable chair to the right of her.

"Would you like some tea?" she asks. "I can ask Lourdes to bring up another cup."

"No thanks, I'm just fine," I say with a smile. "What are you reading?"

"Oh, just some trashy novel," she says dismissively. "It's about a duke or a baron or something, who falls in love with the daughter of his sworn enemy. Honestly, I don't know why I've bothered reading this far."

I suppress a smile. Somehow, I kind of love the fact that I've caught my formidable grandmother reading a romance novel.

"I've not seen you around very much lately, Samantha," Gram says. There's something in her tone I can't quite read, and I'm afraid she's going to start criticizing me. The last thing I want to do today is fight with her, so I turn the conversation to something I'm hoping will make her at least somewhat happy.

"Well," I begin, "I've actually been really busy with a bunch of new clients. In fact, I'm getting so much new business that I'm going to be looking into renting a space downtown and turning it into a photography studio. I need a space to do indoor photos, and I've gotten enough inquiries about things like senior pictures and family portraits that I'm pretty sure I'll easily be able to afford it."

I stop talking, and wait for Gram to start picking apart my idea. But instead, she's still for a moment, and then nods.

"Congratulations, Samantha. That's wonderful news." She gives me a small smile.

I'm so astonished that I can't help but gape at her, but if she notices she doesn't show it.

"I hope that means that you have plans to stay in Tanner Springs," she continues, and takes a sip of her tea. She seems suddenly very absorbed in the bottom of her cup.

"Uh, yes," I stammer. "I think so. For a while, anyway. Business is good, and I like it here."

She nods again. "Good, good." She sets down her cup again, then clears her throat.

"You know, Samantha," she begins carefully, "I did think about what you said regarding the… *plumber* you brought in to fix the kitchen sink."

I tense immediately. Gram and I haven't discussed this at all since the day she was so rude to Hawk. I brace myself for whatever's coming.

"You were right," she concedes. "I was rude. It's just that I was surprised to have… an unknown *person*… in my kitchen. His appearance was… a bit jarring." She looks at me. "I apologize."

Is there something funny in that tea? I wonder briefly. "Well… thank you," I say uncertainly.

"I recognize that perhaps I was too hasty to judge the young man on appearances. Though," she says, sniffing, "I can't say I approve of that death trap he rides around on."

I smile in spite of myself. "I'm sure he'd take that under advisement, Gram," I tell her.

"Yes. Well. Speaking of which," she continues. "I've happened to notice the same *plumber* at the door to the carriage house on more than one occasion."

Oh, no, here it comes, I think with an inner groan.

"He's not a plumber, Gram," I say quietly, and wait for the storm to hit.

"No. I assumed he hadn't been coming to see you to fix the sink in your kitchen," she says with a dry smile.

I feel like a thirteen year-old who's been caught necking in her parents' basement. "Gram," I begin, and then stop, not sure whether I should apologize or try to defend myself.

"I hadn't realized that the two of you were an *item*," she murmurs. "You are, aren't you? An item?"

It's as good a word as any. I resist the urge to laugh at such a quaint word used to describe what's happening between Hawk and me. "Yes, I guess you could say that," I agree carefully.

"I'm not sure whether I ever told you about Richard," she says next. "He and I were an item. After your grandfather."

I risk an admission. "RuthEllen Hanson mentioned him to me once. At the library fundraiser."

Gram's eyes flick to me in surprise. For a moment I'm afraid I've said too much, and that she'll stop talking. But she doesn't.

"I met him many years after your grandfather's death. Richard was a Vietnam veteran. And a professional gambler. Not long after we met, he confessed to me that he had a prison record. From the years after he got back from the war." She looks at me. "I'm sure that when the fine people of Tanner Springs first saw the widow of George Jennings on the arm of a bearded, rough-looking stranger, the gossip was flying." She takes a breath and then lets out a small sigh. "But I loved him. And he me." She pauses. "And unlike my dear departed husband, he never once cheated on me. Nor threatened to strike me." Her eyes glisten. "He was the kindest, gentlest, most loving man a woman could have asked for. I only had Richard for a few years, but every minute was precious to me."

My hand goes to my mouth as I listen to her words. I can hardly believe what she's telling me. For a moment neither of us speaks.

I clear my throat. It's time for a confession of my own. "Did I ever tell you that when you wrote and asked me to come to Tanner Springs, I had just broken off my engagement with a man who was cheating on me?" I ask her.

Gram chuckles softly and shakes her head. "Perhaps poor judgment in marriages runs in the family. Your own poor mother made a similarly bad choice in your father, I'm sorry to say."

Hearing her talk this way about her own son makes me sad for her, but I can't deny she's right.

"Well," I say carefully, "it sounds like eventually *you* got it right." I hesitate for a moment, then reach over and take her hand in mine.

She nods and squeezes it. "Perhaps you have, as well."

Chapter 31

HAWK

"This drive-by can only be the Spiders," Brick is saying during church as he looks around the room. "We've been waiting for them to strike ever since we took back what was ours."

"How the fuck did they choose Hawk as their target?" Angel asks angrily. "Why him?"

Ghost explains his theory that someone from the Spiders must have tailed us on the way back from the Lakeshore. Around the table, the men nod and frown, considering this.

"We've gotta nip this shit in the bud," Angel barks. "Now that they've put a shot across the bow, they're only gonna keep escalating shit until someone gets killed."

"Well, let's make sure it's one of theirs instead of one of ours," Gunner retorts.

"Police are already sniffing around the house," I tell the brothers. "The neighbors must have called them, of course. This isn't gonna be good for the club. Holloway's getting his 'crime problem', and you know he's gonna try and capitalize on it unless we can stop this shit, now."

Eyes look to Rock. He's sitting motionless, lost in thought. He doesn't say anything for so long that eventually a couple of the brothers start to clear their throats. Finally, he opens his mouth.

"Eventually, we may need to take out the head."

The head. The president of the Spiders.

He calls himself Black.

I've never seen him, and I don't know anyone who has.

But as I sit there contemplating his words, I think maybe Rock is right.

And if it comes to that, it may be not only the end of the Iron Spiders, but the end of the Lords of Carnage, too.

Rock ends church by ordering a strict ban of traveling outside the city limits until further notice. We'll continue to take guard shifts outside the club twenty-four seven. All the brothers will do periodic check-ins, and report any unusual activity immediately. Any brother who wants security for his family can stay at the clubhouse or request some of the men to watch over their house. All brothers will keep security video footage from their own houses, and anyone who doesn't have cameras installed at their houses will get them. Samantha and I will stay in one of the apartments here at the clubhouse until the damage to my place is fixed, and until I've updated the security system and gotten stronger locks for the doors and windows.

As we wander out of the chapel, my head is fucking pounding. The club's in a rough spot, and it's only going to get rougher. But that's not why I'm feeling this way.

The club's been in danger before.

But this time, I've got someone else to worry about. Someone other than my brothers.

Since Liam died, I haven't let myself care much about anything. About anyone. Joining the club was a way for me to be part of something bigger than myself. Something where strength and loyalty were all that mattered. The past was irrelevant, and the future was all about my oath to my brothers. Life, death, all that shit — it was all kind of taken care of by that oath. Whether I lived or died was just a matter of whether my time was up. The only thing that mattered was not betraying my club.

But now? Now I've got someone else to live for. Someone else to care about. To worry about. Now, the club's actions don't just affect the club. They affect her, too.

Samantha.

Somehow, she's become more important to me than just about anything. Protecting her is my job. It's my duty. I haven't taken any sort of formal vow, sure. I haven't had her name tattooed on my skin, like I have the name of my club. But she's there, all the same. Tattooed onto my heart.

Back in the main part of the clubhouse, a few of the old ladies are clustered over in a corner. I can't hear what they're saying, but it's clear just from their hushed voices and the worried looks on their faces what they're talking about.

"Have y'all seen Samantha around?" I ask them.

"She left with Jenna a little while ago," Rena tells me. A couple of the other women nod.

Fuck. "Okay, thanks."

In frustration, I head upstairs to the apartment we'll be using for the next few days. Inside, I lie down on the bed and stare up at the ceiling for a few minutes. The memory of being on our date with Ghost and Jenna last night is still fresh in my mind. Sam's smiling face is right there in front of me. I loved how just doing something so normal with her — just going out for some food and a beer with me — made her so damn happy.

Hell, it made me happy, too.

Wanting is dangerous.

I want a future with her. Want it so bad I can taste it. And I want to believe it can happen. But just below the surface — just beneath the fact that I'm happier with Samantha than I've ever been in my goddamn life — there's a black thrum of foreboding. A constant note of danger that I can't ignore. Something isn't right.

I end up falling asleep for a little bit, and when I wake up, my head doesn't hurt as bad. The feeling of danger is still there, though, and I swear softly and sit up on the bed. I don't like having Samantha away from me. Not right now.

I should have told her to wait for me, I think. *I shouldn't be letting her go around by herself right now. I should have insisted on coming with her.*

Pulling out my phone, I check my text messages to see if she's checked in with me. Nothing. I start to put it back in my pocket, then decide I'm going to call her to make sure she's okay. I'm just about to dial her number when I remember the GPS app I installed on her phone and connected to mine this morning. I punch it up and wait for the map to load. The lines start to materialize, and I frown slightly in confusion. It doesn't look like Tanner Springs. Eventually, the design completes itself, and a moving blue dot materializes in the center.

My heart starts to slam against my chest.

Judging from the speed of the dot, Sam's in her car. She's going south.

Right into Spiders territory.

Chapter 32

SAMANTHA

The spot that Annika and Justin have chosen for their engagement photos is out in the country, south of Tanner Springs in an area I've never been to before. On the way down, I drive through a couple of towns of around the same size as Tanner Springs. It's beautiful country down here, hillier and greener. As I drive, I make a mental note to ask Hawk to take me riding down here. I imagine it would be even more beautiful to experience on a motorcycle.

By the time I get to the location Annika gave me, my spirits are lifting and the nightmare of last night feels a little less real. Annika and Justin are already there when I arrive, and I pull in behind their car in the driveway of a rustic farmhouse that almost looks like it's a movie set, it's so perfectly charming.

"Isn't this place *cute*?" Annika enthuses. "It was Justin's grandparents'. His grandma died a couple of years ago, and it's just been sitting vacant ever since."

Annika introduces me to her fiancé, a tall, tow-headed guy who, like Annika, looks like he's about eighteen. He doesn't talk much — clearly, Annika is the more extroverted of the two of them. Annika and Justin are both wearing jeans, matching flannel shirts, and cowboy boots. We walk around the property for a few minutes, scouting locations for photos, and then get down to business. I take photos of them sitting on the ramshackle front porch, on a large log in the yard, out in a clearing filled with tallish grass and wildflowers. The two of them are beaming at each other the whole time, and I'm incredibly happy for them. They're so young and in love, and I silently root for them to be one of the couples who makes it and has a long, happy marriage.

After a couple of hours, I've shot hundreds of photos and we're all starting to get tired. I tell Annika I'll be in touch once I've had a chance to put a gallery together, and we walk back to the cars. Justin's parents live close by and the two of them are going there for dinner, so I say goodbye to them and wave as they pull out of the drive and head south. I stow my equipment and climb in my car for the trip back north.

Since we were going to be tromping around in the grass, I had decided to leave my phone in the car during the shoot so I wouldn't lose it. As I pull my seatbelt on and start the car, I take it from the cup holder and check it for messages. I'm surprised to see that there are over a dozen texts, all but one from Hawk, and three voicemails from him. The first text I see is in all caps, and sends my heart racing in sudden fright:

CALL ME RIGHT NOW

I don't take the time to listen to his voicemails — instead, I choose one and hit "return call" with suddenly shaking fingers. The phone rings once, twice, three times, and I'm preparing to leave a message when Hawk picks up. At first I think the connection is really bad, but then realize the crackling and whooshing sounds I'm hearing are wind and road noise. Hawk must be on his bike.

"Samantha!" he yells into the phone. "Where are you? Tell me you're okay!"

"I'm fine!" I cry. "My God, what's wrong?"

"You're in Iron Spiders territory!"

"What?"

"You're on the turf of the club that did the drive-by last night! You need to get out now!"

My mind races to keep up with him. Hawk hasn't told me much about any of this, and now he's telling me I've driven right into the territory of people who tried to kill us. Trying not to panic, I cry, "Hawk! What should I do?"

"Drive north!" he shouts. "Back the way you came! Do it right now! Don't stop anywhere! I'm coming to meet you!"

I slam the car into gear and floor it so fast I almost lose control on the gravel drive. "I'm driving back the way I came!" I yell into the phone.

"Don't hang up!" he insists. "Drive, but put the phone on speaker and leave it on the seat!"

I don't know whether the threat is immediate, but I've never heard Hawk sound like this. Even last night after the drive-by, he was calm and in control. Right now, he sounds like a man possessed.

It's terrifying.

For a few minutes, I just concentrate on driving, and remembering how to get back the way I came. I'm speeding, but I'm afraid to go too fast because I'm shaking and don't want to run off the road. On the seat, the phone ticks off the seconds of our connection, the sound of the wind and Hawk's engine like a lifeline.

I drive into the city limits of one of the small towns I passed on the way here, and have to force myself to slow down. *I don't want to get a ticket,* I think, and then laugh crazily at myself. The police are the last thing I should be worried about right now.

"What are you laughing at?" Hawk shouts from his end.

"Nothing!" I call out, and feel a surge of momentary relief. It feels good to laugh, even at my own stupidity.

I'm starting to feel a little better now. Maybe Hawk is just overreacting, I tell myself as I pass through the town. Soon, I'm driving through the last traffic lights and accelerating back up to highway speed. "How far away am I from getting back into Lords territory?" I ask Hawk, hoping it's soon so I can relax.

Just as I finish my question, I glance back in my rear view mirror and see four motorcycles pull out of a parking lot at the edge of town.

"Hawk?" I begin uncertainly. "Are you guys behind me?"

"What? No."

"H—how far away are you?"

"Looks like we're about five or six miles out, on the same road as you coming in the opposite direction."

My stomach goes cold. "There are four guys on bikes behind me about half a mile or so," I tell him. My voice rises in fear. "It looks like they have leathers on."

"Fuck!" hisses Hawk. "Floor it, baby! Drive as fast as you can. Don't stop for anything! We're on our way!"

I do as he says, gripping the steering wheel hard as I push down on the accelerator. Glancing in the mirror, I see the motorcycles behind me are getting larger, beginning to close the distance between us. I let out an involuntary shriek and push down harder, praying I can outrun them but knowing I probably can't. My only hope is if Hawk gets to me in time, and if he's not alone. The thought that he might not have brought men to help him brings on a wave of acute nausea, and I try to fight it back as the horrible realization hits me that we might both end up in the hands of the other MC.

What do they want?

Will they hurt us? Hold us hostage? Or…

A loud sob rips from my throat as I push down further, my foot to the floor now. Up ahead, there's an intersection, with a pickup truck about to pull onto the highway. I press down on the horn and pray he won't misjudge my distance and speed and pull out in front of me. I know I won't be able to avoid hitting him if he does.

My car barrels past the pickup, the bikes ever closer. By now I can see flashes of white and red on their vests that I know are club patches. One of the men gestures to the other, and they move into a different formation. They're getting ready to do something. To me.

We come to a fairly steep hill, so steep that I can't see over to the other side. If the bikers behind me are planning to overtake me, they probably won't do it until after we're over it. I jam my foot down to the floor, desperately trying to get more speed out of the car. I'm driving far too fast now, it's not safe and I know it but I don't have a choice. I pray fervently that nothing will be there on the other side for me to hit. The more I consider the possibility, the sicker I feel, as I imagine the crash of metal and the instant death it would mean for me and whoever could be in front of me.

I fly over the hill, my stomach dropping like I'm on a roller coaster, and miraculously there's no one in my path. But now the men behind me are almost on me, and as I glance wildly at them I see one of them is pulling out what looks like a pistol. If he shoots me, or my tires, I'll lose control and I'm going too fast to survive it. "Hawk!" I scream. "Help me!" There's another hill coming up, and as the man with the gun holds it out and levels it at me, I do the only thing I can think of.

I let up on the gas and slam on the brakes.

Chapter 33

HAWK

I'm just opening my mouth to tell Samantha we're almost there when I hear her scream through the phone. "Hawk! Help me!"

The next thing I hear is the squeal of tires, a loud crash, and then silence.

"SAMANTHA!" I roar into my headset. We're not even a quarter mile from her, one hill away, and I throttle up and take the hill so fast that for a second I'm sure I'm gonna fly off the bike. I crest over the top, Brick and Thorn following close behind me, and come down the other side just in time to see Samantha's car skidding to a stop. Behind her, two bikes are tangled together in a sickening heap of twisted metal. Their riders have been flung brutally to the pavement. One look is enough to know that they're both dead. One body is nothing more than a gnarled mess of meat; the other is just bloodied, broken legs sticking partway out of a ditch.

A third bike is smashed into the back of Samantha's accordioned car, I note quickly, and the fourth and last one is riding straight toward us. The leather-vested rider has a gun in one hand, and is tilting crazily and struggling not to swerve and crash.

I fly toward Samantha, knowing Brick and Thorn will deal with the fourth man. Then my bike is on the ground and I'm running toward her car when I hear another crash behind me. I fling open her door, my heart in my throat and expecting the worst. Inside the car, Sam is awake and alive, an airbag stuffed between her and the steering wheel. There's some blood on her face and she's white as a sheet, but other than that she looks like she's okay. She stares up at me, her eyes barely registering me for a moment. She makes a few shapes with her mouth, but no words come out.

"Sam," I croak, kneeling down to her. "Fuck, baby, are you okay?"

She nods dumbly and stares at the airbag in front of her. "I think so," she says in a daze. I take hold of the bag and rip it with my bare hands to deflate it. As it goes down, Sam starts pawing weakly at the buckle to her seatbelt. "Please get me out of here," she whispers.

Behind us, a loud gunshot rings out. I glance back to see Thorn standing over a body, Brick by his side.

"Come on, baby, let's go," I croon, and help her get shakily to her feet. Her eyes are confused, a little unfocused and vacant. She looks like she might be going into shock.

Samantha turns and looks uncomprehendingly at the back of her car. For the first time, I notice that the motorcycle smashed into it has a body attached. Or what's left of one, anyway.

"My camera," Sam murmurs vaguely, and then collapses in my arms.

"She okay?" Brick asks as he comes running up to me.

"She might be in shock," I tell him. "See if you can grab her camera equipment from the back of the car."

* * *

Thorn calls Rock, gives him our location and tells him what just happened. Rock tells him he's going to call Len Baker, Tanner Springs' police chief, and let him know that four Iron Spiders just died in a freak accident just inside our territory.

"Sam, baby," I murmur, holding her in my arms by the side of the road. "We need to get out of here as soon as we can. Are you okay to ride on the back of my bike?"

Samantha takes a few deep breaths in and out. She's trembling like a leaf, but she nods. "Yes. I'm okay."

"You sure?"

She nods again, more definitely this time. "I can do it. I just want to… not be here anymore."

Thorn and Brick drag the body of the Spider that Thorn shot to the side of the road, into a ditch. Thorn comes over to me and lifts his chin toward Samantha. "How's she doing?"

"I'm okay," she answers for herself. "Just… shaken up."

"That was a genius thing you did," he tells her with a half-smile. "Probably the only thing you could have done to stop them."

"Thanks," she says faintly. She shivers and burrows deeper into my chest.

"I need to get her out of here, brother," I murmur to Thorn. "You guys coming?"

Thorn nods. "Not much else we can do here," he says. "What do you want to do with her car?"

"It's toast," I say, which is obvious. "Maybe we should have Rock get a tow truck out here, haul it away."

Brick comes up to stand beside Thorn. "No time for that," he says, shaking his head. "It's a minor miracle no one's driven by here yet. We'll never get the car out of here before the cops see it."

I nod. "You're right. Let's leave it here. I'll have Sam file a stolen vehicle report with the Tanner Springs PD when we get back." It's not a great solution, but it's the best we've got.

"What about the bullet in that Spider's head?" I ask them, glancing over toward the side of the road where his body lies.

"Yeah, unfortunate that," Thorn says regretfully. "I cleaned the gun for prints and threw it down there with the body. There's no way it can be traced back to us." He scans the highway. "Let's just get as far from the scene as possible, and hope for the best."

When I'm certain that Samantha's good to ride, the four of us double back and take a side road toward Tanner Springs so as not to run into any law enforcement on their way to the scene. When we make it back into town, Samantha is still feeling pretty shaky, so I decide to put off having her file the vehicle report until tomorrow.

In the meantime, I'm taking her back to the clubhouse to rest. She's had enough excitement for one day. And so have I.

Chapter 34

HAWK

When I get Samantha back to the clubhouse, she lets me lead her upstairs with hardly a word. She's shaky and exhausted, and all I want to do right now is to get her somewhere she feels safe and can rest. She barely looks around at the apartment, but just lies down on the bed and closes her eyes.

"Don't leave me," she whispers.

I lean down and kiss her softly on the forehead. "I'm just gonna go grab your stuff, baby. I'll be back in a few minutes. You're safe here."

Before long, Sam's drifted off, her face softening as sleep takes her. I go back downstairs and grab her camera bag and the small duffel of clothes Brick grabbed from the back of her car. I haven't had a chance to go back to my place and get anything for myself, but I can't handle the thought of leaving

Sam right now. So instead, I find Thorn and ask him to go by my house for me. There's one thing in particular I need, and I want to have it when Samantha wakes up.

Instead of going back upstairs right away, I decide to grab a beer from the bar and let her sleep for a while. I slump down on one of the stools and motion for Jewel.

"Hey," she greets me, and hands me a bottle. "Looks like you've had a rough one."

I snort softly. "You don't know the half of it."

"I heard about the drive-by last night," she murmurs. "Glad you're both okay."

"I could never have lived with myself if something had happened to her," I reply. The words are out of my mouth before I can stop them, and I'm pissed at myself. I'm not interested in talking about this. I don't know why I said anything to Jewel.

She looks at me for a long moment. "She loves you, you know," she says then. "She's freaking crazy about you."

Goddamnit. "Jewel, I think you're mistaking me for someone who wants to talk about *feelings* with their bartender," I warn her.

She just laughs. "Okay, whatever, tough guy," she says, flicking her towel at me. "You don't have to talk about your *feelings* with me. But I'm just saying, if you haven't told *her* how you feel, I think maybe you should get on that."

I roll my eyes. "What is it with women?"

She gives me a saucy wink. "We're more in touch with our *feelings*. That's what." Her face grows serious. "You *do* deserve her, you know. You're one of the good ones, Hawk."

"Okay, I'm out," I growl, standing up. Jewel's tinkling laughter follows me as I walk away in disgust.

I'm trying to decide whether to go out for a smoke or back up to check on Samantha when Ghost walks in the door to the clubhouse.

"Hey, Hawk?" he calls over to me. "There's some guy outside asking for you."

This day apparently isn't done fucking with me yet. I sigh. "You recognize him at all?"

Ghost shrugs. "Not really. I may have seen him around town somewhere. He's not wearing colors, so he's gotta be a civilian." His lip curls a little. "He looks kind of strung out."

Frowning, I go to the front door and peer outside into the parking lot. The only cage that doesn't belong to one of our guys is parked at the far end. With a start, I immediately recognize it as Anita's car.

Standing next to it, smoking a cigarette, is Anita's brother Tommy.

"What the hell are you doing here?" I growl at him as I walk toward the car. I've probably only had two or three conversations with Anita's younger brother over the years. And every one of them have convinced me that he's even a bigger piece of shit than his sister is.

Tommy holds up his hands in a gesture of submission. "Hey, man, look, I come in peace." He gives me the hint of a smile, but it doesn't reach his eyes. "I just wanted to give you some information, man, and maybe ask a favor."

I can't imagine anything Tommy has to say that I need to know. "Fine. Go," I bark. "I've got shit to do."

His eyes flicker downward for a second, then back up to my face. His gaze doesn't quite meet mine. "I just wanted to let you know about Anita, man. She OD'ed a couple days ago."

Holy shit. "OD'ed," I repeat. "So, is she…?"

"She didn't make it." Tommy shakes his head. "She was alone when it happened, I guess. So no one was around to help her out. They think the H was laced with China White."

I don't know what I expect to feel. Anger, maybe. Disgust. I'm not surprised. Hell, if you'd asked me where I thought Anita would be in five years, I probably would have predicted this.

Still. It all just makes me so fucking sad. She was out of control, and she was a manipulative bitch, and she fucked my brother over. In most ways, I hate her.

But deep down, she was just a messed-up kid that never figured her shit out.

I sigh, overcome by sadness. For her. For my brother. For the stupid kids we all used to be.

"Where's Connor?" I finally ask. I glance over at the car, but it's empty.

"Child Protective Services came and got him when they found her body," he tells me.

"You didn't try to stop them?" How the hell could he let them take his own nephew? I'm fucking furious.

"Hey, I wasn't there, man, all right?" He holds his arms wide in a supplicating gesture. "Besides, maybe it's for the best. I mean, I can't take care of a kid. Connor will be okay, right? They'll find him some kind of foster family, or something. He'll get adopted, right? By some doctor family or something."

Jesus. I shake my head in disbelief. It's true, though. Tommy might even be a shittier parent than Anita was. But isn't there *anyone* in Anita's family who could take him? I can only imagine what Connor's life has been like so far, and now he's gonna be thrown into the system — tossed around from family to family, until maybe, with luck, someone decent decides to keep him. I feel sick.

"So yeah. I thought you'd wanna know…" Tommy trails off, and sticks his hands in the pockets of his jeans. He stands there, not saying anything but not moving. I suddenly remember he said he had a favor to ask.

"So, what's the favor?" I say, pulling out a smoke and lighting it.

"Well… I know you've helped Anita out before," he begins with a hopeful grin. "And I'm kind of in a bind. I just lost my job, and I could use a little cash to hold me over until I find something else."

I close my eyes and take a deep breath, then let it out. Suddenly, I'm fucking exhausted. All I want is to go back upstairs with Samantha, and shut out the rest of the world for a while. When I open them again, Tommy is standing there expectantly. Sighing, I shake my head and pull out a couple of twenties.

"Here," I say, handing them to him. "Thanks for letting me know about Anita."

"Sure thing, man," he says helpfully.

"Don't come back here again," I tell him. "We're done, you understand me? Done."

He looks a little crestfallen, but nods. "Okay, dude. I get you. Thanks for the cash."

I don't bother to tell him goodbye. I just turn back to the clubhouse. I'm more tired than I remember feeling in years. With everything that's happened in the last couple of days, it feels like the end of an era.

An idea starts to form in my head.

And maybe, I tell myself, *just maybe, the beginning of a new one.*

Chapter 35

SAMANTHA

I don't know how long I sleep, but I wake up to the sound of music playing.

I open my eyes to the strange apartment to find Hawk sitting in a chair near the bed. He's strumming his guitar softly, head bent and eyes down in concentration. I don't move, not wanting him to realize I'm awake and stop what he's doing.

The melody is quiet and introspective, and I've never heard it before. I'm not sure, but I think it's something Hawk has composed himself. Lying there and listening to him, it's like I've been given a secret window to a part of him that he keeps closed off from the world. It feels like a gift, and my heart fills to hear it.

The music swells, then slows, and the song ends. Hawk's fingers grow still, and he glances up at me. Our eyes meet, and I smile at him.

"No fair," he murmurs. "You're supposed to be asleep."

"It was a beautiful way to wake up," I say. "I love hearing you play."

Hawk gets up and leans the guitar against the chair, then comes over to sit beside me on the bed. "How are you feeling?" he asks.

"Better." I take a deep breath and look around the room. "Honestly, the whole thing seems kind of like a dream, now that we're back here."

"Good," he nods. "The sooner you put it out of your mind, the better."

"What's… going to happen now?" I ask, not sure how to put all my questions into words.

"You and I will stay here for the time being. We'll wait to get a sense of what the fallout is going to be with the Iron Spiders." He takes my hands in his. "I'm going to protect you, Sam. I promise you. Nothing like this will ever happen to you again." His eyes are fierce, determined.

"I know," I tell him. And I do. In spite of it all, I've never felt safer in my life than I do when I'm with Hawk. It's all I want. *He's* all I want.

"I've been fighting this for a while now," he continues. "I've been telling myself I didn't deserve you. That I needed to stay away from you. But it turns out I can't." He pulls me closer, until the heat of his skin is radiating off him like my own personal sun. "I'm in love with you, Samantha," he growls. "I don't want to pull you into this life if it's not what you want. It's dangerous sometimes. It's not the easiest path. But I can't go any longer without telling you. I want you with me. If you'll have me."

It's the most romantic damn thing I've ever heard.

"I love you, Hawk," I whisper, as my eyes fill with tears. A burbling laugh escapes my throat. "I remember the first time I met you, how I made fun of your name."

"Yeah," he grins wickedly. "And remember what I said in response?"

My cheeks redden. "You said I…" But before I can continue, Hawk's lips come down on mine, firm and insistent. His tongue flicks against my lips, and I draw in a sharp breath and open mine for him. My arms go around his neck of their own power, my skin already electric at his touch. I know what he can do to me. I know what's about to happen.

His hands run up under my shirt, rough against the skin of my back. They're strong, demanding. In control. His fingers expertly flick open my bra, and in one fluid motion, I'm naked from the waist up, everything that was covering me in a heap on the floor. I throw my head back and arch toward him, wanting his mouth on my skin. My nipples grow taut.

"Samantha," he rasps. He pulls me on top of him so I'm straddling him on the bed, my already-soaking mound pressing against the growing bulge in his jeans. I grind myself against him. "Fuck," he groans. His mouth slides down the skin of my throat, burning it with kisses, and then captures one needful bud in his mouth. I moan as the zing of pleasure shoots through me, and grind harder against his length, impatient already.

My hands clutch at his shoulders, my legs going around his waist. There's too much fabric between us, I want it gone but I'm already so wild with desire I can't think straight. I whimper as his mouth closes on my other nipple and he begins to suck and lick. "Hawk!" I gasp. "Oh, God, yes!"

He teases me for a little longer, and then pushes me back down on the bed. He stands and pulls off his T-shirt and his jeans, his eyes a darkening storm. "You're not naked enough," he growls. My eyes not leaving his, I unbutton my jeans and slip them down over my hips with my panties, kicking them off the side of the bed. Above me, Hawk grunts his approval, then takes hold of his large, hard shaft. He slowly begins to stroke it as he gazes down at me. I watch him do it, lust consuming me, and bite my lower lip.

"Fuck," he hisses as he looks at me. "You have no idea how much I wanted to bite that lower lip the first time I met you."

I tilt my head down and stare at him through my lashes, biting it harder.

"You're gonna pay for teasing me like that," he warns.

"Oh yeah?" I challenge. "Do your best."

He's on the bed so fast I let out a little shriek of laughter that turns to a moan when he pulls me toward him and draws one nipple into his mouth again. He sucks them slowly, one at a time, chuckling at my whimpers of need. His lips leave my breasts and begin to work their way down my body. I throw my head back and wait, barely daring to breathe as the ache between my thighs grows more intense. I spread my legs for him, gasping as his thumb grazes over my slick nub. I cry out softly and arch toward him.

"I should torture you," he murmurs, his breath hot against the skin of my thigh. "I should pin you here, so you know how close I am, and not give you what you want."

"No," I whisper. "Hawk, please."

"You didn't take very long to break," he says. "How am I gonna make you pay when you give up so soon?"

"Hawk!" I beg. "Please, make me come. I need you." I buck my hips forward toward his mouth, and he laughs softly and gives me what I want.

The first lap of his tongue is so sweet I almost cry, it feels so good. He begins to lick me slowly, so slowly, knowing exactly where the line is for me between pleasure and agony. I moan his name, my legs opening wider, and it's already starting, I'm already climbing higher and higher, rocketing toward something that's so powerful it's almost frightening.

My whole body is tense as he continues to lick and swirl around the spot that he knows will send me over the edge. Finally, when it feels like every muscle in my body has gone rigid, he plunges his tongue deep inside me and then laps long and deliberately as I scream his name and the most intense orgasm of my life shatters through my entire body.

The waves are still ebbing through me when I feel Hawk's strong hands lifting me up. He flips me over onto all fours before I know what's happening and positions himself between my legs. "I need you," he growls. It's not a question.

"Yes," I say breathlessly. I feel the heat of his cock sliding against my still-sensitive folds and let out a loud moan, closing my eyes as he sinks himself inside me. Hawk's in no mood to take his time now, and begins thrusting hard and fast, deeper and deeper every time we crash together. I grip the sheets, crying out as my pleasure begins to mount again. The velvet heat of him sliding against my puffy lips is so exquisite, so perfect, that before long I know I'm about to come again. I cry out to him and he answers me. "Yes, baby. Sam, I'm so close, baby, I can feel you ready for me. Come with me, baby. Come with me *now!*"

"Oh, yes… *God!*" I scream, shuddering with the force of it as I clench around him. Hawk drives himself into me once more and goes stiff as he explodes inside me with a roar.

I'm still quaking and struggling for breath when I feel Hawk pull out of me and gather me into his arms. He kisses me long, and slow, both of us panting.

"Holy crap," I finally gasp.

"By the way," he tells me between breaths. "I told you so."

"Told me what?" I'm confused.

"The first time I met you. I said you were gonna like my name a lot better when you were screaming it with my head between your legs." He grins at me cockily. "I wasn't wrong, apparently."

I sigh in mock exasperation, even though I want to burst out laughing. "Seriously. Did you set up this whole elaborate plot just so you could get me into bed and prove yourself right?" I ask, rolling my eyes.

Hawk snorts softly, and leans down to brush my lips with his. "Nope. But you gotta admit, we could have saved ourselves a lot of time and trouble that first night if we'd just ditched the wedding reception and gone off to test my theory."

I lean into his hand and kiss his palm. "I know this sounds crazy, considering everything we went through to get here," I whisper. "But I wouldn't have traded it for the world."

* * *

Later, as we lie back against the pillows in each other's arms, Hawk tells me about the visit he had earlier from Anita's brother. I listen in shocked silence as I hear that Anita is dead, from a heroin overdose. Hawk's face constricts as he talks about Connor's being handed off to Child Protective Services, and what that probably means for this little boy who's already had such a hard life, and who just lost his mother.

And then, Hawk asks me a question. It isn't anything I've ever thought about doing, but as soon as he suggests it, I know it's absolutely the right decision. When he's finished talking, I don't even hesitate. I just say yes.

"This is a pretty big thing you'd be signing up for," he tells me. His eyes are dark and serious. "It's only temporary. But are you sure?"

I nod. It's a big step, I know. Probably this is crazy for us to take on, especially so close to the beginning of our relationship. But just the fact that Hawk is asking me to do it with him tells me everything I need to know about whether it's right.

We'll take every day as it comes. We'll struggle, I'm sure. But somehow I know it's what I want. What *we* want.

EPILOGUE

HAWK

"Connor?" Sam says, kneeling down to the little boy. "Do you want to go see some puppies?"

From my vantage point on the couch, I watch as Connor looks at Samantha with wide, uncomprehending eyes.

"Puppies," Sam tries again. "Like your stuffed puppy." She points to the plush dog Connor is clutching against his chest. It was the first toy we got him when we took him home with us. Connor's been holding on to that thing like it's a life preserver ever since.

Connor's been here with us for about two weeks now. We're his foster home until Child Protective Services tells us otherwise. So far, so good, I guess, though it's been a little rough at times. We've managed to feed him, and take care of his needs. But he still seems pretty withdrawn, and a little afraid of us. It's breaking Sam's heart — although she doesn't let him see that.

The process to take him in with us was a lot more complicated than I thought it would be, and for a while I wasn't sure if we were going to manage to convince CPS to let us foster him. Since Sam and I hadn't actually gone through the formal process to be foster parents, the agency was pretty reluctant to consider us as potential caretakers for Connor. Things were looking pretty bleak, until Connor's CPS caseworker got hold of Anita's brother Tommy. Tommy told her I was a friend of the family, and that Anita would have wanted me to take Connor if she was still here to make the decision.

According to the caseworker's records, Connor's a little over two years old. Old enough that he should be talking more than he is, according to Sam's internet research. But so far, all he's done is nod or shake his head when we ask him questions. At least he seems to understand us when we talk to him. It's hard to know what kind of delays he might have, with him having Anita for a mom. From what I witnessed on the rare occasions that I saw them together, she didn't interact with him much.

In the past day or two, Connor's seemed like maybe he's finally starting to come out of his shell a little. So Sam had the idea of bringing him out to Geno's farm to look at the litter of puppies his Shepherd mix just had. It seems clear from the confused way he looks at Sam when she asks him about it that he doesn't quite grasp what a puppy is. But hey, what little boy doesn't like soft, furry things, right? So we buckle Connor into his car seat and drive out to Geno's farm in Sam's new car.

Geno and his old lady Carmen are both home when we get out to the farm. Carmen takes us out to the barn, where their dog Molly is with her pups. Inside, it smells like hay, manure, and animals. Somehow it's always struck me as a clean smell, even though I guess that doesn't make a lot of sense. It smells uncomplicated. Soothing.

Molly and her litter are in an old refrigerator box that's been laid on its side and had the top two-thirds cut off it so the lip is just tall enough the pups can't get out. Old blankets line the box, and inside, seven wriggling puppies squirm around and bite at their siblings' ears and paws.

I'm carrying Connor, and I kneel down and set him on the ground beside me. His eyes are wide and astonished as he takes in the scene before him. Sam picks up one of the puppies and holds it out so Connor can touch it. Gingerly, the little boy reaches out a tentative hand and pats the little animal's fur, then pulls it back quickly.

"See? It's a nice doggy," Sam says in a soothing voice. "His fur is soft, isn't it?" Sam pets the squirming puppy to show Connor. "We pet him very gently because he's just a little baby."

Connor reaches out his hand again and pets him like Sam showed him to. He looks up at her questioningly, and she smiles and nods at him. Suddenly, he does a little half-hop and squeaks with excitement.

"That's the mommy dog, right there," Sam says, pointing. "These are all her little babies. Aren't they cute?" Connor squeals again, a little louder this time.

"Doggy!" he says with a wide, grin, pointing toward Molly.

Her eyes fill with tears. It's literally the first word he's spoken since we got him. "That's right, sweetheart," she whispers, glancing at me. "It's a doggy."

We stay in the barn for a long time, letting Connor watch and pet the puppies. He's almost unbelievably gentle with them. Finally, we decide it's time to let Carmen and Geno get on with their day.

"You know," Carmen says with a twinkle in her eye as we leave the barn, "We're going to be looking for homes for most of the puppies. You have first dibs if you want one." She smiles at Connor. "A dog is a boy's best friend, after all."

Sam looks up at me, the beginnings of a smile on her face. "We'll think about it," I say firmly. Hell, we've only had Connor for two weeks, and now we're already talking about getting a dog? This whole domestic bliss thing is happening a little fast for me, even though it was my idea to take Connor in. Hell, next thing you know we'll be putting up a white picket fence.

"Okay, Connor, we're going to go back home now," Samantha tells him. "We'll come back very soon and visit the doggies again."

"Pet the doggy!" he says again, joyously.

Sam laughs. "That's right. Wave goodbye to the doggies and Carmen!"

Amazingly, he holds up his hand and flaps it in their direction, smiling shyly.

"Bye-bye, Connor!" Carmen says as she waves back.

"Do you want to walk, buddy?" I ask him as we leave the barn. "Or do you want me to carry you?"

Connor looks down at the ground for a minute, then up at me.

Then he holds out his arms.

"Okay, buddy," I say, trying to ignore the sudden rasp in my throat. "Carry it is."

On the way home, neither of us says much. Sam turns on some bouncy kid's music she found online for Connor to listen to. A couple of times she sniffles quietly into a tissue.

"You okay?" I finally ask, reaching out for her hand.

"Yeah." She glances back at Connor, who's fallen fast asleep in the back, and then shoots me a tearful, tremulous smile. "I think maybe he will be, too."

I know Connor isn't my brother's kid. I know there's no connection to Liam beyond the same hot mess of a girl that just never managed to get herself together.

But even so, somehow I still feel like the universe has given me a second chance. A way to do something good, to atone for my brother's death.

Sam seems to understand this.

That's one of the countless things I love about her.

We haven't talked about adopting Connor, either. Not exactly. But I think that's the direction we're heading in. It's early days, of course. There's no guarantee we'd even be chosen to be his new parents.

But when I think about the future, the hazy image in my mind is me, Sam, and Connor. And maybe another little boy or girl.

If it's a boy, I hope his name is Liam.

Sometimes, late at night, I lie awake and try to figure out whether life is just fucking with me. Everything seems too perfect right now. Sure, the war with the Spiders is far from over — that's a story for another day.

But right here, right now, I feel like I can conquer the world and face anything that comes, with Samantha by my side.

She's the woman I want to be with, for the rest of my life.

And for once, what I want is exactly what I have.

BOOKS BY DAPHNE LOVELING

Motorcycle Club Romance

Los Perdidos MC
Fugitives MC
Throttle: A Stepbrother Romance
Rush: A Stone Kings Motorcycle Club Romance
Crash: A Stone Kings Motorcycle Club Romance
Ride: A Stone Kings Motorcycle Club Romance
Stand: A Stone Kings Motorcycle Club Romance
STONE KINGS MOTORCYCLE CLUB: The Complete Collection

GHOST: Lords of Carnage MC

Sports Romance

Getting the Down
Snap Count

Paranormal Romance

Untamed Moon

Collections

Daphne's Delights: The Paranormal Collection
Daphne's Delights: The Billionaire Collection

ABOUT THE AUTHOR

Daphne Loveling is a small-town girl who moved to the big city as a young adult in search of adventure. She lives in the American Midwest with her fabulous husband and the two cats who own them.

Someday, she hopes to retire to a sandy beach and continue writing with sand between her toes.

Printed by Amazon Italia Logistica S.r.l.
Torrazza Piemonte (TO), Italy